Café
Conversations

SHORT STORIES BY MARION REIDEL

ISBN: 978-1-988215-69-3

Author photo: Trina Koster Photography
Cover Art: Write Design
Editing: The Indie Editor

Library and Archives Canada Cataloguing in Publication:

Reidel, Marion, 1955 –
[Short stories, Selections]
        Café Conversations/Marion Reidel

Layout and Design by One Thousand Trees
www.onethousandtrees.com

Printed in Canada by M&T Printing Group
Guelph, Ontario

First Edition, 2019

Dedication

This collection of stories is dedicated
to neighbourhood coffee shops where people
gather and their life journeys intersect.

Brenda + Donna

Cheers to my budge

buddies. Thanks for

your support.

Mauri

Acknowledgements

My gratitude to Lisa Browning at One Thousand Trees Publishing for her faith in my work and support of this project.

Thanks to Jeremy Luke Hill, and Vocamus Press, for leadership of the Guelph writing community. His constant efforts to build networks and celebrate wordcraft are invaluable.

A special thanks to my dedicated group of Beta Readers: Susan Andrews, Kathy Gemin, Sheila McLean, Janet Mersey, Margot Mouret, and Jean White. Their patience, thoughtful feedback, and encouragement helped me reach the finish line.

Contents

Is That You?   1
The Company We Keep   5
Celebrating Crones   9
I Quit   17
Frenemies   23
Disability   31
Blind Date #1   37
Phobia   47
I Remember   51
Transformation   57
Drinks With Mother   63
On the Contra   69
An Epidemic   75
The Diagnosis   79
Useful Information   87
I'm Listening   95
Late-Life Speed Dating   101
No Try There Is   127
The Red Dress   133
Blind Date #2   139
That Particular Grandmother   141
Hidden Motive   145
Like a Mole on Your Ass   149
Blind Date #3   157
They're Trying to Kill Me   161
Good Advice   169
She's a Landmine   175
Watch What You Say   183
Blindsided   189
Writer's Craft   195

Is That You?

"Is that you?" Lisa leaned over the table, causing her T-shirt to reveal a bare shoulder upon which a tattooed wasp perched.

"Huh?" The bearded man she addressed continued moving the stroller adjacent to his left thigh as he looked up from his latte to assess the tousled woman.

"It's me, Lisa. Oh my God, you have a kid? I was going to comment on the beard. Love it. Right on trend. Very urban lumberjack. But . . . a kid. Is it yours?" Lisa settled herself. "Okay if I sit here?"

"Uh, yeah."

"This seems like a nice place. Conversation Café, I guess that means we better talk, huh?" Lisa placed her tote bag on the table. It was woven in bright geometric colours that suggested indigenous Central American design. She purchased it on Etsy. A cluster of trendy buttons embellished its surface. Some of the slogans included, Chocolate Inspector; Free Tuition; Take My Advice— I'm not using it; and, I stalk myself on Facebook.

She bent down to see the infant more clearly. "What's it's name? Is it a boy or girl? Not that gender matters. How old are *they*?"

"Uh, her name is Emma. She's eight months."

"She's ahhh-dorable. Oh my God. Ginger hair just like yours. Hey, you know what it's called when a ginger loses their temper? A Ginger Snap!" Lisa laughed. "It's *so* good to see you."

"Mmm, thanks . . . ah."

"I never see *anyone* from high school anymore. Do you? I guess it's just one of those things. You know. People we thought were the centre of our universe move on, lose touch. I try to keep track of people on Facebook. Some people closed their accounts or something. I don't know what's up with that. They just disappeared from my list. Like they got sucked into a black hole."

A staff member in a crisp white blouse and short black skirt delivered Lisa's latte saying, "Double shot, vanilla with soy."

"Thanks. So . . . who's Emma's mom?"

"Paula Wilson."

"Are you married? Not that traditional marriage is a requirement for procreation. That's such an antiquated idea, don't you think? Where'd you two meet?"

"At university. Are you—"

"Yes! Yes! Yes! I found the love of my life. Thanks for asking. I guess you won't be surprised when I tell you that I'm a lesbian. I think *everyone* suspected in high school. It only took, like, a bazillion failed heterosexual relationships for me to get it. I was probably the last to know. Ha! But really, I don't think people fall in love with the gender. You know what I mean? Don't you agree? I fell in love with the person. She just happens to be a bitchin' hot babe." Lisa smacked her hand on the table, laughed, and pulled the drooping T-shirt neckline back on her shoulder.

The outburst startled the baby. Her father inserted a soother.

Lisa leaned over the baby, again. "My lover's name is Jasmine, and yes, she's delightfully Indian just like the Disney princess. I'm living the fairy tale. She's like . . . salted chocolate. We're deliriously happy together. She's the reason I'm back in town, actually. I swore I'd never return, but Jasmine got a job with that rehab place, Addictions R Us." Lisa chuckled. "Not really. I just call it that. It's got some corporate name, the Harding Institute for Rehabilitation of something or other. Jasmine is recovering, herself. Designer drugs, you know. Her personal experience really helps her connect with the inmates. She's a very kind and caring individual. Nothing at all like me. Ha!"

The man picked up his fussing daughter and bounced her on his knee. "So, Lisa, I can't—"

"Oh my God, you make amazing babies. Seriously, you could start a stud service. Check out that face. Aren't you the little cutie? Yes, you are. Yes, you are." Lisa reached to stroke the baby's cheek, and the child began to squeal.

"Uh, thanks. Listen, I—"

"You know, that's the only drawback of being a lesbian. The ole baby-making process. Missing a key ingredient. Ha! You know what I mean?" Lisa took a sip of her latte.

"Sure. High school, you say?"

Emma sucked on her soother as she pulled at her father's beard.

"Those were the days, weren't they? We thought we could conquer the world. I was going to be a famous actress, then reality hit when I had to pay my own bills. Speaking of which, I bet having a kid is pretty expensive."

"Well, yeah . . ."

"You must have a good job."

"I'm a lawyer."

"Ooh. How exciting. I can imagine you in court defending accused innocents."

"I handle real estate and family law, mostly."

"Oh, like adoptions and stuff." Lisa reached out and caressed Emma's fuzzy head. "You sure make beautiful babies. Jasmine and

I are considering going to a clinic . . . but it's really expensive . . . and there's no guarantee. And you don't really know who the sperm donor is. I mean, you can pick the ethnicity, and they tell you something about the man's education, so you get an idea of his intelligence, but really, it's a gamble."

Emma's tiny fingers got tangled in her father's beard, eliciting a wince from him as she tried to withdraw her hand.

"Maybe I'll just nab a kid, eh? Emma's such a cutie. Would you like to come home with me, Emma? Would you, sweetie? It would be easy to make off with a little one. When they're that young, they'd never remember their real parents. I wonder how often that happens."

Emma's father tugged her close to his body. "It's every parent's worst nightmare."

"Listen, this may sound really random, but, seriously, have you ever considered being a donor? People are prepared to pay a lot for a sample. And what does it cost you? Nothing. A few moments of pleasure, actually, eh? What do you think, Tom?"

"Tom? Who's Tom? My name's Nathan."

The Company We Keep

"Wow. This place is busy today. Just a minute, Jade. A medium latte with skim milk, please. Yes, *sedici*. That's what I meant. The middle, sixteen-ounce size. No whip, thanks. I said skim milk. Skinny, non-fat. My name is Cyndi, C-y-n-d-i. Thanks."

"Are you still there, Jade? Did you hear that? Did you? Geez, I purchased cars with fewer questions. I know. I know. I know. I usually go there, too, but I was feeling restless so I thought I'd go a little farther afield. Are you still at work? Of course I've got my laptop. I'm as keen as you are."

"Here. That's mine. Thanks."

"Hang on a minute, Jade. Just a sec, this place is crowded. I need to find a table."

"Excuse me, sir. I beg your pardon. Sorry to bother you, but is anyone sitting there? Thanks. Would've been polite if they cleared their table, eh? Some people."

"I'll call you right back, Jade. I've got to clear my own table."

"Sorry to bother you. I hate to be a pest. Can you watch my laptop for a sec, please? Stupid people. Can't even carry their mugs to the cart. Ick. What is that sticky stuff? Crap. Where are the paper napkins? Honest to God."

"Thanks again. Hey, do you mind plugging me in? There's an outlet behind your feet. Thanks a lot. I really appreciate it. You're the best. That's it. Okay. I'll leave you alone. Cheers."

"Hi, it's me. Sorry about that. I'm just turning my computer on now. No. I'm at a place called Conversation Café. Yeah, that's the one. It looks cute. Comfy furniture, dark wood panelling, some local artwork on display. Paintings mostly. I don't know. Seems like acrylic. Graphic images. Lots of colour. Nice. Okay, my friend, I'm up and running. What's the web address? How'd you find out about it? Really? I thought you didn't care for her. Ha. Ha. At last, her bragging pays off, eh? Okay, got it. Oh my God!"

"Sorry. I didn't mean to be so loud."

"Holy smokes, Jade. The cabins are right out in the water. I adore the turquoise shutters and . . . look at that . . . it shows a glass floor in the living room. I'm going through the photo gallery. You can see right down into the water. It's lit up and everything. Cripes! It's gorgeous. Fantastic. Amazing. It says fifteen hundred per night. We can't afford that."

"Are you sure? What if she was exaggerating? Can she be trusted?"

"Who are these international businessmen? Do they even speak English?"

"No. I'm still interested. I have a passable knowledge of Spanish, but I don't know any Portuguese. I just want to be clear about what I'm getting into."

"So, all she did was socialize with them. Dinner, dancing, drinks . . . no sex, right? Don't lie to me, girl."

"Yes, I wanna cheap holiday. Cheap is good, but I don't want to sell my soul for it. If these Brazilian millionaires want the company of blond North American women, that's great, but—"

"Ha. Ha. No, I don't need a middle-aged Latino husband, you idiot."

"So, what'd she say *exactly*? Tell me the truth. Fess up."

"That counts as sex."

"No, I can't talk any louder. I'm in a café for heaven's sake."

"Listen Jade, a BJ counts as sex."

"Yes it does."

"Does so. Ask anyone."

"Fine, in my opinion, a BJ counts as sex, and I'm not prepared to do that for a free holiday. I don't care how beautiful the place is."

"Yes, I saw the private hot tubs . . . and the hammocks overhanging the water . . . and the swim-up bar. Listen, there's no question, you're absolutely right. It's the most beautiful place I've ever seen."

"The food damn well better be gourmet."

"Well . . . I'm prepared to engage in charming conversation and dance with them. I'll stroke their egos, but I'm not stroking anything else."

"No. I will *not* stroke that. Listen to me—"

"No. Never. Absolutely not. Listen, Jade. I'm serious."

"What you're talking about is not escort work. It qualifies as prostitution. Jade. Jade. Listen. People are starting to look at me strange. I gotta go."

"Yes, it seems fabulous . . . amazing . . . heavenly."

"I know. I know. I know. But there's got to be a limit, a set of ethical standards, a line that must not be crossed."

"Well, she's lying, then, because there's no way she got a week at that place without putting out in some manner. Not a chance. Impossible."

"Okay, I'll sleep on it. Let's talk later. Give me a ring tonight."

"Yeah, I'm gonna make the resort picture my desktop image. Can't hurt to dream, eh?"

"Love you, too, kiddo. Talk later."

Marion Reidel

Celebrating Crones

"I don't like this." Marg looked Dorothy directly in the eye. "I wouldn't want it done to me."

"But Annie's not like you . . . and we're not doing anything *to* her. It's a celebration of her eightieth birthday. Women need to embrace their maturity, Margaret."

"You mean getting old and grey."

"Silver hair is a badge of honour. I call it Arctic blond. And lines on one's face are an indication of a life fully experienced." Dorothy stirred another envelope of raw sugar into her tea. She loved the golden crystals offered at the Conversation Café.

"You listen, Dorothy Wilson. I have a very expensive moisturizing regime. I work hard to avoid wrinkles." Marg unconsciously elongated and stroked her neck.

Dorothy smiled as she assessed the creased corners of her companion's eyes and mouth. "I think wrinkles add character. A blank face looks like one of those robots in the movies. An aged face is interesting. Women are living longer, and the notion that they're dried-up and useless is a thing of the past." She took a sip of her tea.

"No one considers Annie useless," said Marg. "You know full well she's a hospice volunteer. It's really important work." She lifted her coffee mug and added, "And if wrinkles are so acceptable, then why are there so many anti-aging products?"

"You're an expert at detecting life's inconsistencies." Dorothy chuckled while she stirred her tea needlessly and gazed out the window. She, Marg, and Annie, had been friends for decades. They raised their children together and wrapped Annie in their embrace when her husband died. Although Marg got crustier every year, Dorothy knew she had a soft heart. "Let me tell you about the crone party. It's based on the ancient belief that female elders are healers, teachers, and keepers of the tribal history."

"Obviously, Annie taught history for twenty-five years. Some of her students still—"

"I don't mean it literally. I'm talking about ancient Wicca traditions."

"Wicca?"

"The worshipping of nature and the mysteries of life from before people created organized religion and politicized everything."

"Annie loves going to church."

"Women are claiming the name crone in a positive way just like the gays embrace the word queer and rappers use . . . the N-word."

Marg gasped. She checked to see whether adjacent customers had reacted to Dorothy's vocabulary.

"It's paganism, darling." Dorothy took another sip of her tea and watched for her friend's response.

"Paganism? You mean dancing naked around a bonfire and offering sacrifices? We're all Protestant. Don't expect me to put on a hooded cloak and offer up a black cat."

Dorothy laughed. "Don't worry. There'll be none of that."

"Good thing. We've done a lot of goofy things over the years but . . ."

Together the women giggled as each retreated into her own treasured memories for a moment.

On the café's sound system, Sarah McLachlan sang, "Ice Cream," a calm song quite at odds with the moment as two young mothers with noisy toddlers bumped Marg's chair while trying to settle at the next table.

Dorothy continued, "The crone ceremony is a tribute to the final stage of a woman's journey. Just because a woman is no longer able to bear children doesn't mean she offers no value to the tribe."

Marg took a deep breath. "Okay. Tell me exactly how it works."

"Well . . ." said Dorothy, leaning forwards and continuing in a hushed tone, "a high priestess oversees the ceremony. I asked Audrey Cookson to play the role. She owns a gold lamé evening coat and a beautiful tribal necklace she bought in Costa Rica. Plus, she's going to the party store to purchase a feathery masquerade mask. She'll look totally authentic."

"Mmm."

"We'll begin with a ritual bath to purify Annie and rid her of any negativity. The party will be at my house, so we can use the hot tub. We'll place lots of candles and those tiki torches around the patio."

"Is this a nighttime event?"

"Oh yes. Don't you think everything is more powerful when done in candlelight? Elise Watkins is going to do a guided meditation. Did you know she's a certified yoga instructor now?"

"No."

"She'll amaze you. She can chant in Sanskrit and everything. It should be extremely moving."

"How will we understand what she's saying?"

"It doesn't matter. The language sounds beautiful and exotic. The emotion in her voice will be clear. Elise has community theatre experience. She'll do a fabulous job."

"If you say so."

"When Annie emerges from the hot tub, naked of course, we'll put a cloak over her shoulders, well Henry's silk bathrobe, actually, and we'll place a tiara on her head."

"A tiara? Like a beauty queen? That doesn't sound ancient."

"I know. I know. It's supposed to be a floral garland, which would symbolize Annie's love of her garden, but she also likes glitzy things, so I think we should get a rhinestone tiara from the bridal shop."

"I see."

"There will also be drumming. Elise, Pat, and that friend of Audrey's belong to a drum circle." Dorothy finished her drink. "I had another great idea."

"Do tell."

"Pat and I took belly dancing last spring. We still have the jingly belt and scarves. We could do a belly dance to the drums."

"Let me see if I completely understand what you're saying." Marg placed one elbow on the table and rested her chin on her hand. "You're going to invite the members of our bridge club—"

"And the hospice volunteers."

"Okay, the bridge club and the hospice volunteers will come to your back yard, which will be lit by candles and torches, and we'll watch our eighty-year-old friend exit from your hot tub . . . naked—seeing her climb out of there should be an attractive sight—then, you're going to dress her in your husband's old bathrobe and a fake tiara so your neighbour, wearing a 1970s evening coat, a souvenir necklace, and a Halloween mask can bless her while a bunch of old white women bang on African drums and dance around with a retired accountant mumbling something in a dead language."

"We also need to burn some herbs, probably sweetgrass, to further sanctify the space. And there'll be a celebratory meal with lots of wine. We'll organize a potluck. Audrey makes the best lasagna in town, and Debbie's Caesar salad is to die for."

"Gee, could we howl at the moon? Or perhaps, I don't know, maybe sing something . . . like Happy Birthday, maybe?" Marg sat back, pleased with her sarcasm.

"Don't be silly. Of course we'll sing, and we can give her crone gifts."

"I'll bite." Marg sighed. "What's a crone gift?"

"That store downtown, the one with the crystals and incense, also sells mugs that say, Crone Power and T-shirts with Elderpower and Crone Club logos. There are amulets and books of inspirational sayings. Lots to choose from. There are even joke gifts like dead roses or a hat with a black veil."

"But Dorothy, you said the point was to celebrate aging, and now you're talking about classic gags. You're being contradictory."

"My goodness, Marg. You take everything so seriously." Dorothy shook her head. "I just want to create a special event for our pal. She's the first one of us to hit the momentous mark of eighty. I thought a crone party would be fun. No matter what I suggest, you manage to pick holes in it. This happens every single time, and I must tell you, it exhausts me. Can't you be supportive, for once?" Dorothy finished her tea and set the cup back on the saucer with a clatter.

"I'm sorry, Dot." Marg reached across the table and patted her friend's hand. "It's obvious you put a lot of thought into this. I'm just worried the plan is a little over the top. What if Annie isn't comfortable?"

"But Annie's the one who suggested it."

"Really?"

"She read about it in *Modern Seniors Magazine*."

"And she liked the idea?"

"She thought it was exciting. She told me all about it. So, I looked it up on my computer and got the details."

"Okay, then. If you're sure Annie will enjoy it, let's do it." Marg noticed one of the children from the next table staring at her as she sat back in her seat. She gave the child a wave, and he quickly turned away.

"There's just one more detail," said Dorothy.

"And what's that?"

"The naming ceremony."

"Explain."

"It's a pagan tradition to adopt a magical name. The crone could choose it themselves, or it can be given to them by the priestess. I thought it would be meaningful to give Annie a spiritual name for her birthday."

"What did you have in mind?"

The child stared again, so Marg made a face, and he turned away.

"Well, in the Wicca tradition, the terms *Lord* and *Lady* are used for elders, so I thought Annie should be Lady something."

"That sounds nice."

"We should think of something important to Annie like her garden or her hospice work."

"Lady Hospice? Lady Gladiola?" Marg smirked.

"Something a little less obvious. Lady Caring, Lady Care, Lady Kindness, Lady Comfort."

"Lady Comfort sounds like a prostitute."

"Honestly, Marg, how does your mind work?"

"How about Lady Rose for those bushes along her front porch? Or Lady Hyacinth? That sounds pretty."

"I wonder if we could do a combination to capture both aspects of her. Lady Gentle Rose, or Lady Compassionate Rose."

"You know, I like that. Lady Compassionate Rose. That's our Annie," said Marg, leaning forwards and smiling. She felt a gentle tickle of excitement.

"Lady Compassionate Rose. It does sound lovely, doesn't it?"

"It does." Marg let out a sigh. "I'm sorry I fought you on this, Dot. I think Annie will love the whole thing. You're a good friend."

"Thanks. I'll call the girls and give them their assignments." As Marg finished her coffee, Dorothy smiled and said, "When you turn eighty next year, we'll name you Lady Prickly Thorn."

Marion Reidel

I Quit

"I quit my job today."

"What? I can't believe that you'd make a decision like that without consulting me." Richard glared at his wife as she avoided his eyes and sipped her drink. "After thirty-two years of marriage, I thought you'd discuss it with me." He looked at the reflective black surface of his coffee, then scanned the crowded café. "Listen, I have to get back to my office in twenty minutes. Let's talk this through tonight."

"I felt trapped."

"My God, Helen, everyone feels trapped!" Richard snorted. "That's what life is like for grown-ups. We accumulate responsibilities, the mortgage, tuition, car payments, credit card bills. You can't just up and quit your job. That's ridiculous!" Richard observed a pair of old ladies sitting in the front window. Both turned his way. One held a yellow teapot suspended above her cup; another had frozen mid-sip. He lowered his voice. "You're just having a bad day. Things will seem better tomorrow."

"The monotony is mind-numbing."

Richard thumped his forehead with the heel of his hand. "Monotony? You chose to become an accountant. You claimed to have a passion for numbers. You like the girls at work. You said your boss values you. You got a bonus at Christmas. Honestly, I can't understand what your problem is." He spoke in a controlled tone.

"I'm tired all the time."

"Sweetie, everyone's tired." Richard leaned back in his chair and smiled. "Let's buy that new mattress we've been talking about, one of those memory foam things. If you get a better night's sleep, you'll feel more energetic. And we can renew our gym memberships. Exercise gives you more energy. I realize that your knees are bad, but you can do the water aerobics. Lots of gals your age enjoy that kind of thing. It would be fun."

"I dread going to work."

"So? Do you think I leap out of bed in the morning?" Richard chuckled. "Work is what we do during the day so we acquire the resources to enjoy our lives. We've got a beautiful home, new cars, and our kids are attending reputable universities. We took a holiday in the Caribbean last winter. What the hell more do you want?" He didn't bother mentioning the five-dollar latte his wife was drinking. Richard took a deep breath and admired a new painting on the wall opposite him. Usually, he enjoyed the friendly buzz of this downtown café.

He turned back to his wife, who was cradling her designer beverage. "Listen, there are a lot of people with real problems. Jake Patterson got laid off after forty years. Bruce Wojcicki's wife ran off with his neighbour. Ah . . . Tony Costello's teenaged daughter is pregnant, and Dev Hassan's wife's cancer is back. Those are real troubles, Helen. They're not just sad and tired. You need to suck it up."

"I no longer recognize myself."

Richard snorted. "Are you kidding me? Christ Almighty, I don't know what to say to that." He raised his arms in a gesture of defeat, then promptly dropped them to avoid attention. "You've read too many women's magazines or watched too much *Oprah*." He shook his head and let out a long breath. "You no longer recognize yourself? Perhaps that's because of your complete wardrobe turnover in the last year. You spent hundreds of dollars on those bright, glitzy tunic tops. There's another reason why you need to keep working. There are things in the closet with the sales tags on them."

"I'm getting old."

"Yeah? Well that's how life works as long as you're living. I don't have time for this." Richard shifted his mug, spilling coffee on the table's battered surface. "Take a breath. Talk to your boss, and tell her you need to take a leave of absence. Explain that you're burned out. Maybe you can go and visit your sister for a couple weeks. Talk this through with her. She'll help you realize it's foolish to walk away from such a desirable job. Here's an idea . . ." Richard reached across the table and took his wife's hand. It felt limp and clammy between his rough fingers. "I'll find a counsellor. A professional who specializes in mid-life crises. Someone who can help you work through these feelings and get you back on track. We've worked too hard to build a comfortable life. You gave three decades to that company. It doesn't make sense to toss it away." He withdrew his hand and used it to prop up his jaw.

"I want to do something of value."

"It's work, Helen!" Exasperated, Richard glanced around, adjusted his volume, and continued in a harsh whisper. "It's employment. They wouldn't pay you if it wasn't valuable. If you want to save the world, adopt a starving orphan, volunteer at the Literacy Centre, go hug a tree for God's sake, but don't cut our family income by forty percent."

"We've built exactly the life we wanted." He continued in a subdued tone. "You remodelled the house to be precisely the way you want it. The kids are on their way. Your folks are off in Florida, and we finally can enjoy all the freedom in the world. The only requirement is doing the work that generates the revenue to sustain our lifestyle." A knapsack struck Richard on the side of his head, without apology, as a bearded youth settled at the next table.

"I want to find my creativity."

"Great." Richard sighed and checked his watch. He took hold of his mug but set it down when he realized it had lost its warmth. "Helen . . . sweetie . . . you're very creative. All you need to do is take a course at the Rec Centre. They teach scrapbooking, painting, pottery, photography. Find a hobby. Meet some new people. Have some fun—but do it after work hours. Okay?"

"My life is slipping away."

"Honey . . . Helen . . . my love." Richard sighed. "Our life is perfect. You and I are exactly where we wanted to be. We've got everything we wanted. We're both driving new cars. The cottage renovation is done. We got the powerboat and our home theatre. We're living the dream." Richard made eye contact with his wife and noticed a tear toppling over her left lid. "You know what this is, don't you? You just turned fifty, and you're having a mid-life crisis. It happens to everyone. There's no need for you to feel ashamed, sweetie. You'll get over it. Trust me."

"I don't know where I'm going."

Richard drew in a deep breath and let out a sustained sigh. "You're going with me." He attempted a weak smile. "We're travelling together down the road of life. We're partners, contributing to a shared dream, and that's why you must keep working. We can't sustain our lifestyle on my income alone. Think about it realistically. Imagine what we'd need to give up if we lost your salary." Richard scanned the room for a clock.

"And be honest with yourself. How long would it take before you got bored? You think you want to quit work, but that would lead to isolation. You'd miss your friends. There'd be no reason to get out of bed in the morning. Without a career, you'd be lost."

"My spirit is dying."

"Now you're being silly. Spirits don't die. They're eternal. They outlive your body for heaven's sake. Maybe this is depression? You should go see a doctor and get some medication. What do you think?" Richard touched his phone and checked the time. He placed his palms on his forehead while he watched his wife silently weep.

"I feel like running away."

"Honestly, I have to get back to work. How about I call your office and tell them you're not feeling well? Your boss will understand. You can count on her to be discreet. I'll explain that you're having a little meltdown and you need some time off." Richard picked up his cellphone and scrolled to find the number. "Did you resign in writing or speak to her directly? If you left a letter, she might not have seen it yet. We could pretend it never happened."

"I don't want to surrender. There's got to be more to life than accumulating things, Richard."

"I agree. We've discussed travel plans. What? Why are you making that face?" *Ping!* Checking his phone screen, Richard gritted his teeth. "Shit. I'm scheduled for a meeting in ten minutes. I need to get back. You picked really bad timing for your crisis, Helen. Let me tell Sharon that I'm on my way," he said as he tapped his phone. "Of all the days . . . I can't take time for this." His phone to his ear, Richard turned away from his wife and looked out the window, past the old ladies who were still yacking. "Sharon, I'm running a bit late. I'll be there in . . . eight minutes. I'm leaving now. If he gets there before me, make him a coffee and bat your eyelashes at him. Yeah. That's my girl. Thanks." Richard pocketed his phone. When he turned around, his wife's chair was empty. Through the window, Richard watched Helen walk away.

Marion Reidel

Frenemies

Their friendship devolved into hatred so intense her only options were fight or flight.

"I'm only in town for two days," said Andrea. "My mother is having an eightieth birthday tomorrow, and her pals are throwing her a crone party. Personally, I think they're all nuts."

Jennifer, who had known Andrea since high school, inspected her companion's animal-print, spiked heels. With Andrea seated, the added height was not apparent. She noticed a missing button on her own cardigan. "I never heard of a crone party," she said.

"Of course you haven't, you sheltered thing, you." Andrea played with the stem of her wineglass and glanced around the café. "Have you and Cam done any travelling since last we talked?"

"Not really. It's challenging with the kids being so young. Cameron got a great new position at work. It's taking up a lot of his time."

"Dan and I just got back from Munich. He presented his paper on the triggers for male sexual dysfunction to an audience of eight hundred international psychologists."

"That must be very hard for Daniel." Jennifer smirked.

"Of course not. He's done lots of presentations." Andrea took the elastic out of her hair and redid her blond ponytail as she continued to speak. "They videotaped it for YouTube. You and Cam should check it out."

"Sure . . . sounds fascinating." Jennifer caught herself chewing her bottom lip, an adolescent habit that she hadn't engaged in for twenty years. "And how about you, Andrea? Is work going well for you?"

"Work's a bore. Life's a bore. You understand how it is."

"Not really. My days are busy chasing after Amy and—"

"Oh my god! Isn't childcare the ultimate bore? If I had a kid, which I won't because it totally destroys your body, but if I did . . . I'd hire an au pair to raise it. Changing diapers and cleaning vomit is too gross. You would know, of course. And the teens . . . well, that's a nightmare, too, I hear."

"If it's your own child—"

"Naturally, you have the right to your own opinion even if it's wrong." Andrea laughed. "I suppose that you and Cam haven't accumulated the resources to travel even if you didn't have the kids holding you back. Am I right, or am I right?"

Jennifer forced a smile and took a drink of coffee. It was challenging to make herself available for this meeting. Why did she bother?

"Germany was fabulous," continued Andrea. "The wine was delicious, and the architecture was beautiful. We stayed at the Carat Haus Apartments. Everything was *uber modern*, lots of polished white surfaces and minimalist décor. Their buffet featured fresh fruit and vegetables. Lord knows, I wasn't about to eat the greasy German food. Seriously, sausages are so disgusting."

"I'd love to go to Germany. My great-grandmother was German."

"Gosh, I hope she wasn't a Nazi. Their history is so twisted. I mean, really, master race? You should see the people in Munich.

They are just as fat and dumpy as our middle-class rednecks."

Andrea took a drink of wine, creating a pause that made Jennifer feel she was expected to speak. "I guess people are the same everywhere."

"Listen, Jenn, speaking of the overweight middle class, I can't help but notice . . ."

Jennifer clenched her jaw.

"Well, since you had kids, you've packed on a few pounds. I guess being home makes the refrigerator too accessible." Andrea made a pouty face.

"It's hard. Although I seem to be on the move all day, it's not what one would call a cardio workout. You look fabulous, though. How do you stay in shape?"

"Don't try to change the subject, Jenn. You always do that when we're discussing something you find uncomfortable."

"I do not."

"You do so. Remember at summer camp when we shared a cabin with Patti and Sharon? We all wanted to talk about what it would be like to be a lesbian, and you kept trying to get us to talk about stupid boys from school?"

"Well . . ."

"And remember the time you and Cam rented a cottage with Dan and me. We were drinking, and the conversation turned to open marriages. You tried to get us to watch a rom-com."

"That's not the same."

"It is. I could give you a hundred examples of when you tried to redirect the conversation because you were uncomfortable with the subject. You don't like anything that challenges your small view of the world."

"Now you're just being mean, Andrea."

"The truth hurts, but facing it is the only way we can better ourselves."

Marion Reidel

"I guess I don't share your view of what's true." Jennifer concentrated on keeping her voice steady and tone light.

Silence settled between the women as they sipped their drinks. Jennifer caught snippets of conversations around them. Two young women at the next table discussed their lecherous boss. A couple on their other side debated options for a house purchase. An attractive man in a business suit, seated behind Andrea, spoke to someone on his cellphone while looking at forms.

"So . . . did you buy anything in Munich?" asked Jennifer.

"See, you're changing the subject." They avoided each other's eyes and took another drink. "I'm concerned about your health."

The young women at the next table erupted in laughter then began to gather their things to leave. One bent behind Andrea's chair to pick up a fallen object.

"Does this belong to you?" The woman held out a turquoise scarf with a seashell motif.

"Oh . . . my god! Thank you so much! That's my brand new silk Valentino. I would've died if it got ruined. You literally saved my life," Andrea gushed as she retrieved the wayward cloth.

"No worries," said the woman. Jennifer saw her whisper to her friend on the way out, resulting in a flutter of laughter.

Andrea wrapped the scarf artistically around her neck, a skill Jennifer tried, yet failed, to acquire. "Funny you should ask if I purchased anything in Munich. All the high-end designer stores are there. I got this scarf and these Gianvito Rossi pumps." She waggled her foot. "A stylist told me that leopard print shoes are an essential part of any wardrobe. These ones are hand finished with the perfect pointed toe."

"They're so tall. They can't be comfortable," said Jennifer.

"Are you kidding? They feel made for me, and the heels are only three inches. Honestly, they're a very basic shoe. I can wear them with jeans or out for the evening. I adore them, don't you?"

"Do you mind if I ask how much they cost?"

"They were a bargain. Here they cost over twelve-hundred dollars but I got them for only nine-hundred euros." Andrea brushed a speck of debris off the toe of her shoe.

"But, isn't the exchange rate one point five?"

"I don't know. I don't use actual money. I put everything on my credit card." Andrea started to rise. "I'm going to get another wine. How's your coffee?"

"I'm fine, thanks." While Andrea left to fetch her drink, Jennifer texted her husband, Call in 15 pls, then set her phone face down. She wondered how many hours, days, weeks, months of her life she'd wasted on this relationship. She struggled through the mental math when Andrea, an imposing figure, nearly six feet tall, returned to her seat. Her tight skirt confined Andrea to petite steps. Her posture was regal, her figure perfect, and her face flawlessly crafted.

As Andrea approached, the man on his cellphone looked up. "Andrea?"

She froze, her cheeks flushed as she turned to the man. "Garret? What're you doing here?"

He rose and gave Andrea a formal embrace and peck on the cheek, taking care not to disturb her glass of wine. "I'm here to see a client who moved to a retirement home. He can't come in for a consult, so I went to him."

"Well, aren't you sweet. I hope it went well." Andrea turned and reached to pull out her chair.

The man gallantly helped her into her seat. "Can I join you for a minute?" He gathered his things and sat before she could answer, then turned to Jennifer. "Hi. I'm Garret Armstrong. I worked with Andrea at P&P Capital Investments."

Andrea jumped in to say, "This is Jenn. She and I are school besties. I'm in town for my mother's birthday."

"Oh, I didn't know you grew up here. Nice town." The man fidgeted in his chair and had trouble keeping eye contact. "Listen, I just wanted to say how sorry I am about everything."

"It's nothing, Garret. Don't mention it." She checked her phone. "Shit. Look at the time." She took a gulp of her wine. "I didn't realize the time. I need to head out."

"But you just got a refill," said Jennifer. "So, Garret, you and Andrea work together at P&P?"

"Well . . . we did."

"Jenn doesn't need to hear about our office politics, Garret. Spare her, please." Andrea squirmed and struggled to cross her legs.

"Sure." He placed his hand on Andrea's arm. "I really need to ask . . . have you found another position yet?"

Jennifer watched her companion's carefully crafted sense of importance begin to unravel.

"I've been travelling, actually. Dan was working in Europe."

"You guys are back together?" Garret sat back and smiled. "That's great, kid. I'm very happy for you."

"My break from work is good for us." Andrea began tapping her perfectly manicured nails on the table's surface. "I'm thinking of doing more travelling."

"Right you are. Don't be in a hurry to get back into the rat race, eh? Capital management isn't for everyone. Losing a job can be an opportunity in disguise."

"Of course," said Andrea. She drained her glass.

At that moment, Jennifer's phone rang.

"What's up?" asked her husband.

"Oh, hi sweetie. I'm here having a drink with Andrea."

"Ahh. Did you need a rescue call," his voice whispered into her ear.

"I'm not sure when I'll be home, sweetie. Andrea and I are having a lovely visit." Jennifer smiled across the table at Andrea and Garret, who quietly conversed about mutual acquaintances.

"Okay. You tell her I need you home immediately if you need to be rescued," Cameron told his wife. "I love you, Jenny. You're the light of my life."

"I love you too, sweetie," whispered Jennifer. Then she set down the phone and returned to the drama that is Andrea. "So Garret, how long have you been with P&P?"

"Andrea and I started about the same time, right?"

"Jenn's not interested in this." Andrea reached for her glass.

"Are you kidding? I'm extremely interested." Andrea leaned in and smiled. "Life at home with two little kids is so boring compared to the world of high finance. Gosh, they make TV dramas about your kind of work."

"Yeah. I love it," said Garret.

"Speaking of work, we mustn't keep Garret." Andrea turned and offered her ex-colleague a smile of practiced sincerity. "Don't let us keep you."

Jennifer also addressed him. "I think your concern for Andrea is lovely. Lots of people dump colleagues when they leave the firm." Jennifer kept her gaze on Garret while she monitored Andrea in her peripheral vision. "It's sad when people are treated unfairly, don't you think?"

"Absolutely. I didn't believe the gossip for a minute." He turned and placed his hand on Andrea's shoulder. "I told them you'd never do such a thing."

"Good for you, Garret." Jennifer made a congratulatory gesture. "It's important to stand by friends. Even if they do make choices contrary to ours, everyone should determine their own destiny."

"I couldn't agree more." Garret nodded. "There are lots of people at P&P that shouldn't be throwing stones because their glass houses need window cleaning."

"Oh jeez, look at the time." Andrea flashed the face of her

phone at her companions.

Tension rippled along Andrea's jaw. "And gossip seems to grow. What starts out as a reasonable incident becomes this giant fantasy."

"Like that telephone game." Garret chuckled. "Each time the story is repeated, it gets embellished. That's why I knew that Andrea didn't have an affair with Old Man Parker. It's ridiculous."

"Totally," agreed Jennifer.

"I hate to break up the party, but I really need to be somewhere." Andrea gathered her things and rose. "It was great to see you again, Jenn. Give my regards to . . ."

"Cameron."

"Of course, Cameron, and the kids." Andrea blew a kiss across the table. "Take care, Garret. What a surprise to run into you here." They shook hands. Both Jennifer and Garret silently watched Andrea's backside sway as she wove her way out of the café.

"What a wonderful coincidence that we ran into you, Garret. Do you have time to stay and chat?"

Disability

Abby leapt up to move a chair out of the way. She set it beside the entrance to the washroom, leaving a tiny gap so the chairback would not bang against the wall.

"Thanks for letting me share your table. I love this café, but it's pretty hard to get in to."

"Yes, it's very busy. It seems particularly crowded today."

"No. I mean literally. It's physically inaccessible. There's no ramp at the entrance and no power button on the door. I can manoeuvre this chair pretty well, but they sure could make things easier." The young man's smile shone from his mahogany complexion. "My name is Bhisham." He reached out to shake Abby's hand.

She took a deep breath and gave his fingers a quick squeeze. His skin was distinctly warmer than room temperature. "I'm Abby. Nice to meet you."

A server approached to take Bhisham's order, a black coffee and gluten-free cookie. Abby had a letter *H* indicating that her order was pending. They chatted pleasantly about the good weather. The server returned quickly, bringing both orders at the same time.

"You live in this neighbourhood?" asked Bhisham. He noticed

Abby discreetly wipe the spoon with the hem of her shirt.

"Yes." She turned her cup so the handle was projecting ninety degrees to the right, carefully stirred her latte, so as not to cause any foam to spill into the saucer, then set the spoon on it at a forty-five-degree angle. "I was born in town and did all my schooling here. My parents live ten minutes away, and my grandparents are in a retirement home at the north end of town."

"I've only been here for three months," said Bhisham. "I like living downtown. I don't drive, for obvious reasons, and so it's nice that there's a market, drugstore, and liquor store all within a two-block radius. And, I gotta say, city buses that kneel are pretty great."

Abby knew she was expected to contribute to this social interaction. That's why she'd challenged herself to share the table. A raggedy bit of skin on her left thumb was tormenting her, but she didn't want to bite it off in front of this stranger. "I like it here very much," she said. "I have an apartment by the main branch of the library. I've lived there for"—she did some mental calculations—"three years and seven months."

Bhisham laughed. "Well, Abby. You're very precise." He thought her curly hair, freckles, and furrowed brow were adorable. "What do you do for a living? No, let me guess. You're an accountant."

"No."

"A bank teller?"

"No."

"A hairdresser?"

"No."

"A taxi driver?"

"No."

"A welder?" Bhisham smiled.

Abby was concerned that he was laughing at her. She felt her stomach clench, and the voice in her head told her to run away. She regretted inviting him to join her, but it was too late to change that decision. "I'm a copy editor at Harlequin Publishing."

"Cool. Do they have an office here?"

"No. I work at home." She fiddled with the ragged cuticle under the table. "Files are sent electronically, so editors can be anywhere in the world."

"As long as they have Wi-Fi and speak English, I guess." Bhisham dunked his cookie in his coffee.

Abby was not sure whether this was a statement or question, so she waited for Bhisham to speak again. She pictured the mushy cookie crumbs that would accumulate in the bottom of Bhisham's cup. She shuddered as she imagined how they would feel when the final mouthful of coffee was consumed.

"Harlequin. They're famous for romance novels, right?"

"Harlequin publishes women's fiction in a variety of genres. Some of the categories are, Action and Adventure Romance, African American Romance, Body, Mind and Spirit, Biographies, Christian Fiction, Cozy Mysteries, Crime Thrillers, Erotica, Fantasy Romance, Gothic Romance, Historical Romance, Inspirational Suspense, LGBT Fiction—"

"Okay, you've made your point. They publish a much wider range of . . . literature than I thought."

"Of course, I don't edit African American or LGBT because I'm not qualified to do so."

"But you are qualified to edit erotica and crime?" Bhisham laughed but realized from his companion's facial expression that she didn't understand he was joking.

"I mainly handle language conventions and continuity issues. Occasionally, I have to research whether or not the content is realistic."

"Interesting." Bhisham decided not to make a comment about researching erotica.

Abby was not drinking her latte. She was concerned that it might cause a foam moustache. She decided to initiate a new topic of conversation. "What caused you to be in that wheelchair, Bhisham?" She sat back, linked her hands in her lap, and rubbed her other thumb against the irritating skin flap. She felt confident that his response would fill in a significant amount of time.

"Broke my back in a skiing accident. A tree jumped out in front of me when I was travelling eighty kilometres per hour." He continued to dunk his cookie.

Under the table, Abby tugged at the skin on her thumb. It seemed to have grown larger and more ragged. "That's unfortunate." The loose skin wasn't quite long enough to grasp with her fingers, but she knew her teeth would tear it off in a second. She thought she could do it quickly the next time he looked down to dunk his cookie.

"Yeah, I was pretty miserable at first. I was really into extreme sports. You know, dirt biking, rock climbing, that sort of thing. My parents made me go to counselling. I hate to admit it, but that helped me to adapt to my new circumstances." He took a drink of coffee then wiped his mouth with a paper napkin. "I still work out. Upper body only, naturally. It takes strong arms to move this thing all day."

"You could get an electric one," suggested Abby.

"They're too big and clumsy. This rig serves me well, and my apartment is specially modified, so I'm totally independent. Well, except for crowded cafés, but then the benefit of that is being asked to sit at a pretty girl's table."

Abby made full eye contact for the first time. "Do people often ask you to sit with them?"

"Well, no, actually," said Bhisham. "This is the first time."

"But you said—"

"I was joking." Bhisham dunked his cookie and tried to think of a conversation topic. When he looked up, Abby quickly withdrew her hand from her mouth and put it below the table. "Is there something wrong with your latte?"

"No."

"It's just that . . . you haven't touched it."

Amy dropped her left arm to her side and picked up the cup with her right. She took a sip of latte, taking great care not to tip it too high and thus cause a moustache. When she set it down, she suddenly raised her left arm and let out a tiny shriek.

"What's wrong?" Bhisham leaned forwards to see her hand.

"I'm bleeding." Amy tried to hold the hand as far away from herself as possible.

Bhisham picked up his napkin, reached across the table to take hold of Amy's wrist, and gently drew her hand towards him. He wrapped her thumb and applied slight pressure. "It's okay. I've got this. Relax. I can help you."

Marion Reidel

Blind Date #1

She said she'd be wearing a red coat. Alisa . . . Ah-lee-sha, Ah-lee-sha. Oh man, I don't want to say it wrong. It's 7:03. She's late. Maybe she's not coming.

A petite woman in a red coat enters the café with her hair tucked into a toque, so I can't see the colour. Why is she ordering a coffee? She should look for me first. I wanted her to sit down and let me get her coffee. Shit! Should I approach her?

I don't want to lose this table. I came thirty minutes early to snag a table for two with a clear sightline to the door. My jacket draped over the back of the chair will hold the table for me. I've got to intercept her before she orders. Why didn't she scan the café when she entered?

I slide out of my seat. As I approach the line at the cash, the petite red coat turns and looks right at me. Oh, my gosh! She's gotta be fifty. I freeze in my tracks.

"Miserable night out there, eh?" The petite red coat smiles.

"Uh, yes, uh, I was just going to the bathroom," is my incoherent reply. What the hell? Is there some reason why I should explain to this stranger, who clearly is *not* Ah-lee-sha, why I'm out of my seat?

I turn away from petite red coat to head towards the bathroom, as I promised the woman I would, when another red coat comes through the door. She pulls off her hat and shakes out long amber hair. Stamping her high-heeled boots on the mat, she looks around the café until her blue eyes come to rest on me.

"Hi there. You wouldn't happen to be Benjamin, would you?" This new red coat smiles.

"Ah-lee-sha?" I reply.

"That's me." She stamps a couple more times, then steps forwards and shakes my hand. Her fingers are freezing. Her long oval nails are bubblegum pink.

"Uh, our table is over there." I lead her five steps and gesture to the table where my coat hangs limply. It's not as if the route requires complex navigational skills. "What would you like to drink?"

"Gosh. Give me a minute." She begins to struggle with her coat, and I snap into action.

"Here, let me help you with that." I step behind her to assist with the removal of her coat and give it a shake to dislodge the snow. What I think is a gallant move gets me a dirty look from two middle-aged ladies who receive the spatter.

I hang Alisa's coat on the back of her chair and make an effort to slide the seat under her as she takes her place at the table. She places a large purse at her feet and sets down a cellphone wearing a case encrusted with "jewels."

"You must be freezing. What can I get you?" I ask.

"Gosh. How about a latte?"

"Okay." I turn to go and place the order.

"Made with almond milk."

I pause. "Oh . . . okay."

"A double shot, please," she adds.

"An almond milk latte with a double shot of espresso," I clarify.

"And a flavour shot. What's your favourite?" she inquires.

Is this a test to check my competence and compatibility? "I don't take flavour shots in my coffee," I reply. "But there are lots of choices."

"I'd like vanilla. And gosh . . . I'm really hungry. Would it be alright if I had their double chocolate toffee square?" Alisa smiles up at me, her head slightly tilted to her right, and places the index finger of her right hand on her chin.

"Of course, whatever you want. An almond milk vanilla latte with a double shot of espresso and a double chocolate toffee square coming right up." From my place in line, I covertly assess my blind date. Her back is facing me, and a waterfall of glossy amber hair falls to her shoulder blades. Her eyes were a startling shade of blue like that energy drink that tastes like berries.

An almond milk vanilla latte with a double shot of espresso and a double chocolate toffee square. An almond milk vanilla latte with a double shot of espresso and a double chocolate toffee square. I rehearse her order in fear of making an error and being judged inattentive. When I place the order, I get a standard latte for myself. I read somewhere that matching a date's preferences is perceived as desirable. I also order an oatmeal cookie so that Alisa won't be eating alone and thus feel gluttonous. The whole order cost almost fifteen dollars. I sigh and shake my head as I drop seventy-five cents in the Thanks a Latte tip jar. I guess I'll be having Kraft Dinner twice this week.

I carry the two plates back to the table along with a sign bearing the letter Q to identify the pending drink order. As I approach, Alisa finishes sending a text and sets her phone down.

"Here you go." I carefully place the dessert in front of her, the cookie at my place, and the sign in the centre of the small table. I worked as a waiter during my first year at university and know how to carry a plate and set it down respectfully.

"Gosh. Am I supposed to eat this with my fingers?" Alisa strikes a coy pose as she awaits my response.

"I'm an idiot. Just a se-second, and I'll get you some cutlery," I sputter.

"And a napkin, please," Alisa calls as I depart.

I return to the table with napkins and two sets of cutlery. I didn't know that people eat dessert squares with a knife and fork. Will she think I'm rude if I eat my cookie with my fingers? A *Seinfeld* episode flashes through my brain in which people eat chocolate bars with a knife and fork. I let out a little chuckle as I set down Alisa's cutlery. Shit! I hope she doesn't think I'm laughing at her. Should I explain? She'll think I'm crazy. Besides, I hate people who constantly reference *Seinfeld* episodes. "There you go, Ah-lee-sha," is all I say.

"Thank you, kind sir," is her adorable reply. She does indeed begin to eat her square with a knife and fork, in tiny bites, imperceptibly diminishing its mass. After a brief discussion of the evening's weather, she says, "So, you're a friend of Greta's."

Okay, an invitation to conversation. I can handle this. "Yes, we're in the same Biology lab section. We're working on a llama dissection together. It's a fascinating process, removing each layer, fur, then muscle, to expose the internal organs. We pretend we're doing important surgery and that we're going to save the life of our patient, Larry, when in reality, he died of old age. Apparently he was . . ." Alisa is paused with her fork suspended in mid-air. "Is something wrong?"

"Gosh. It's just that . . . well . . . perhaps we could talk about something different. Something a little less gruesome." She smiles and tilts her head.

"I'm sorry." I'm an idiot. "I love veterinary medicine so much that I sometimes forget that shop talk is not socially appropriate." Thank goodness the server appeared with our orders.

"An almond milk vanilla latte with a double shot of espresso?" asks the server.

"That's mine." Alisa mimes silent applause.

"And the latte for you, sir. Will there be anything else?"

"Ah-lee-sha?" I ask.

"No. I'm fine, thanks."

"Enjoy," says the server as she takes away our *Q*.

"W-well then . . ." I stammer, trying to restart the conversation. "How do you know Greta?"

"She's in the same residence as me, two doors down. We don't really hang out, actually, but the other day, a bunch of us were sitting around bitching if you'll pardon my French . . ."

"Of course." I smile and nod.

"We were bitching about how there are no decent men around. For example, I was dating a football player who's an absolute Neanderthal. He never wants to talk. He doesn't read literature. The only movies he likes are action pictures. It was impossible to relate to him."

"I see."

"So, we're all sharing stories about the obnoxious guys we dated, and Greta mentioned you."

"She did?" I never dated Greta. She has a boyfriend back in her hometown and no interest in replacing him. Why would she mention me as an obnoxious date?

"She's a big fan of yours."

"Really?"

"Gosh, yes." Alisa pauses to sip her latte. "Greta said you were the opposite of every guy we described. She said you read and can carry on a real conversation. Honestly, it was like a sales presentation." We both laugh. "So I said, Greta, you really must to fix me up with this dream man. And here I am." Alisa makes a little gesture to indicate, ta-dah.

"That was kind of Greta. I guess she thought we'd have something in common," I say.

"Gosh, no." Alisa laughs and places her hand on her cheek. "In fact, she tried to discourage me. She said we were opposites, but I told her opposites attract. That's a known fact. My outgoing personality will balance your shyness."

"Greta said I was shy?"

"Not really shy, just a bit socially awkward. I think that's adorable. I'm tired of good-looking confident guys. I'm ready for the introspective, sensitive type. I think it would be wonderful to have a boyfriend who puts my needs ahead of his own."

I realize my mouth is hanging open as I struggle to form an appropriate response to this statement. I hear Justin Bieber whine about unrequited passion ... It's Alisa's ringtone.

"Excuse me. I need to take this."

I nod my approval and pick up my cookie with my fingers.

Alisa turns sideways in her seat, averting her eyes and holding the phone to her opposite ear as if this creates an invisible wall through which I'm unable to hear her conversation. I drink my latte and act deaf.

"Hey. No, I can't right now. No. Because. I'm not at home. Never mind. It's none of your business. I don't need to tell you my plans. Listen, I'm busy. I'll talk to you later. No. I'm hanging up now. No. I won't. Don't be such a baby. When? Okay. Bye." Alisa sets her phone face down on the table.

When she turns back to me, my hearing is restored. "Sorry about that. A needy friend." She sips her latte. "Don't you hate it when people make unreasonable demands on you?"

"Well I . . ."

"I mean, gosh, we all must take responsibility for our own decisions, right?"

"I guess . . ." I'm not exactly sure what she's referring to or what response might be correct in this situation. I'm still distracted by being referred to as socially awkward.

Alisa launches into a lengthy monologue on the trials she faces from people who demand her wisdom and support. These constant impositions seem to revolve around fashion decisions and the borrowing of various items of apparel. She holds her opinions in very high regard and makes it clear that many of her peers depend on her intervention to establish or sustain their social standing.

I discover Alisa's comments blending into the white noise created by the surrounding conversations. I maintain eye contact and nod when there's an appropriate pause or when her inflection indicates a request for agreement. I drink my coffee and consume the cookie while I notice that Alisa is no longer eating her $2.80 square.

Greta was right. This girl is no match for me. Greta is a true friend. Too bad she's committed to that long-distance relationship. Wow, Ah-lee-sha doesn't need to breathe between sentences. She does have beautiful eyes. What is that shade of blue? Not as purple as cornflower, nor as turquoise as an algae bloom. I've seen that blue on tropical fish. Almost iridescent, as if she's a robot.

"Don't you think?" she asks.

Shit! Don't I think what? "Well, I-I'm not sure," I respond hesitantly. I stroke my chin and choose a pensive expression.

"Of course, how would you know? Silly of me. You're such a patient listener that I completely forgot I was talking to a man." Alisa offers a conciliatory smile.

What does she mean by that?

"It's just that when we women are on our period, hormones totally destroy our ability to think rationally, and so, it honestly should be a legitimate consideration for needing an extension for assignments or exams. Trust me on that."

Yikes, is that what she's been talking about? "That's a very interesting point, Ah-lee-sha. How's the double chocolate toffee square?" I inquire.

"Gosh. It's delicious, but it's just soooo big. I can't possibly finish it."

"They could put it in a box for you to take home," I suggest.

"I don't think so. I shouldn't eat that much sugar, anyway."

Then why did she order the damn thing?

"Do you want to finish it off?" She pushes the plate in my direction.

There's a trap question if I ever heard one. If I say yes, I'll look like a pig. Shit! She's nibbled ten cents worth of the damn thing, and she used a fork. It's not as if it's contaminated. "No. I ate my cookie," I reply. Time to change the topic. "So, you like to read. What's your favourite book?"

"Gosh. I'm a rabid reader. Once I start a book, I just can't put it down. I adore the *Shopaholic* series. I read six of them. And . . . they made a movie. Are you familiar with them?"

"No."

"You'd love them. The stories are funny and poignant. This girl, Rebecca Bloomwood, is some kind of journalist that's supposed to advise people on how to manage their money, but in fact she . . ."

White noise. I can't even check the time because my phone is in my pocket. Smile. Nod. What the hell is this girl talking about? I thought she said she liked literature. And how about conversation? I think her take on that art is a little one-sided. Smile. Nod. *Gosh*, get me out of here.

Look at her jaw working. I wonder what it would be like to dissect a human being. A corpse is a corpse. It shouldn't be much different from a horse or llama except without the fur. Smile. Nod. If I opened Ah-lee-sha's cranium, I wonder what would be in there.

"Gosh. Listen to me doing all the talking." Alisa pulls me out of my dream state. "How about you? What's your favourite book?"

"Favourite? That's hard. I'm an avid reader and—"

"I know what you mean." Her phone vibrates, and she flips it over to view the screen. With an exhalation and flick of her finger, she dismisses the message. "I could go on about lots more books, too. We could spend all night comparing our favourites like this."

Like what? She hasn't let me finish a thought.

"Gosh. It's been really nice, Benjamin." She reaches for the bag at her feet. "You are such a good listener. We really must do this again sometime."

"Mmm." That was noncommittal, right? There's no bloody way I'm investing more time and money into this relationship.

Her phone vibrates again, and she checks the screen. "Being needed is such a burden." She offers a well-rehearsed smile, then she pushes her seat out to rise.

I hustle over and assist with her red coat. Her hat falls to the floor, so I retrieve it and hold it out to her.

"Thanks again for a lovely evening, Benjamin," Alisa says as she accepts the hat.

"You're most welcome, Ah-lee-sha," I reply.

"Call me." She waves as she departs. I see her begin tapping the screen of her phone as she heads out the door.

"Mmm," I murmur and wave to the back of her red coat. I sit down and pull her plate to my side of the table.

I signal the server who is clearing adjacent tables. "May I have a take-away box for this please?" I ask, pointing to Alisa's brownie.

She's the same server who brought our coffee. How can her blouse and skirt seem so fresh after a long day in this place? She fetches the container quickly and makes eye contact as she offers it to me. "I hope everything was okay." She smiles as she clears the table.

"I have faith that it will be."

Marion Reidel

Phobia

Each morning brought a new battle. Physical aches inhibited movement, so she snuggled under the warm duvet. The air temperature, several degrees cooler than her cocoon, tormented her sensitive skin. Goosebumps formed as each hair on her body became an exclamation mark.

The desire to withdraw went beyond physical sensations. Voices, like an unruly crowd within her mind, created a constant chatter that demanded heed to the countless awaiting dangers. Something sharp on the floor, poised to pierce the tender flesh of her instep. A deadly toxin hidden in her bathroom among instruments meant to cleanse and comfort. Electrically charged wires, scalding liquids, tainted food, all lurked within the heart of her home.

Beyond the boundaries of her residence skulked psychotic strangers, killer vehicles, rabid animals: a gauntlet of hazards that must be faced daily to get to the safety of her workplace. Rousing herself required so much energy, exhaustion became her constant companion.

Her appearance went beyond tidy. Each layer tucked—white top and black bottom. A stain would be debilitating. She avoided mirrors. Egocentric imperfections refused to let the day proceed until their needs were addressed.

* * *

Rituals brought comfort and kept the risks at bay. Touch the doorknob three times; use the left hand railing; step over the mat; sit on the edge of the chair; let the water run for sixty seconds; insert the toast top-end first, and never drink the last of the orange juice.

If her preferred seat on the bus was taken, she'd stand as rigid as the pole she dared not touch, mentally radiating a protective force field around her.

At work, routines were essential. She loved the perfection of the coffee bean grinder, which she kept immaculately clean. Tamping the grounds and ensuring a level surface before locking in the group head felt joyous. The precision of the brew timer and the symmetry of the flow calmed her as did the choreography of steaming milk and filling the vessel. Washing hands was the best routine of all, undertaken hundreds of times each day.

Only in the café could she escape the internal voices. The wash of noise created by the patrons' animated conversations drowned the nagging within her mind. The busier the environment, the better she felt. No time to think; just do the coffee dance.

* * *

The café's customers comprised her unwitting social network. Although invisible to most of them, she knew the habits of the regulars, caught snippets of their lives through overheard conversations. She observed their body language with precision sufficient to identify how their days were going.

The trio of grannies was among her favourites. She loved the forthright manner in which these long-time friends conversed. Abrupt or unguarded comments did not cause offense. They always sat at the same table by the window. The cranky one liked the yellow teapot. The little one always wore pearls. The third one had watery blue eyes framed by thousands of laugh wrinkles. As she passed, a mixture of floral scents, a combination of perfume, hand cream and herbal tea, made their table smell like a garden. They always greeted her with a cheery, "Hi Kate," and asked how her day was going. She sometimes fantasized that one was her own grandmother with whom she might discuss her dreams . . . and fears.

She found the couples fascinating. From her place behind the counter, she could tell whether it was a romantic liaison, business meeting, or breakup. A touch of a companion's hand could be foreplay, compassion, or condescension. The minuscule variance did not escape her perception.

Then there was the boy, Benjamin. He sat alone, working on his laptop. Isolated by earbuds. He seemed so shy, yet he always made eye contact, never failed to express appreciation. He met a girl the other night. An awful girl. She had to resist spilling a drink on his chatty companion. It appeared to be a date, but they departed separately. Her loss.

In the café, a single voice sometimes rose above the chatter. "I won't put up with it any longer!" "Please be honest with me!" "How can you accuse me of such a thing?" Customers discreetly paused their conversations, leaning tactfully towards the disruption. Patrons avoided direct stares in favour of oblique glances. Everyone loves drama, and the café always had plenty to serve.

* * *

In the evening, darkness infiltrated her home with the stealth of a spider. It crept silently behind her shoulder until it saturated the room. Lights intentionally left off, no need to create a fishbowl to entertain neighbours. She felt her way to the stairs; climb on the left side; touch the open door's handle; fold clothes symmetrically before placement in the laundry basket. The ache returned as she slipped under the duvet, body heat captured by down, pillow caressing her neck, voices whispering their warnings.

I Remember

"I remember being excited about my prom dress, then finding out the meanest girl in the graduating class was wearing exactly the same thing." Sylvie recalled the teenaged trauma.

"I remember putting my hand up in class and never being called upon." Bernice raised her hand as she spoke.

"I remember sitting alone in the school cafeteria, feeling sure everyone was whispering about me. My God, high school was a jungle." Sylvie smiled and shook her head. "I remember neither one of us fit into the cool group."

"Ha! I can top that," said Bernice. "I remember attending business parties with Derek and being introduced as 'the wife.' For that matter, I remember the other preschool mothers calling me Ricky's Mom, never my own name."

Warm laughter wrapped around the two old friends and blended with the chatter of the café's customers. It had been five years since they'd sat in the warmth of each other's company.

"I remember the whole family forgetting my forty-seventh birthday because their favourite team was in the World Series," countered Sylvie. She couldn't recall the name of the team, but she knew it was baseball in October. Sylvie gazed adoringly at Bernice drinking coffee. She'd changed externally but was still the same precious friend. "Must you leave on Friday?"

Bernice smiled and set down her mug. "Yes. I can only hide from reality for so long." She took a deep inhale and slowly let out her breath. "Hey, here's one for you. I remember Celeste Worthington introducing herself to me at the Country Club even though we'd met three times previously."

Sylvie laughed. "I remember being too uncoordinated to keep up with the step-box class. Even when I was in the back row where I could see everyone."

"That's true. I'm your witness." Bernice shook her head as she pictured their spandex bodysuits with high-cut legs, beige tights and colour-coordinated sweatbands.

"Oh . . . oh . . . how about this one? I remember at my daughter's wedding, her new mother-in-law telling a friend I was overweight. She didn't realize I was in the bathroom stall and could hear her every word. That was brutal. It's amazing how her marriage survived such an evil woman."

"What's really amazing is how many of my humiliating stories include you." Sylvie's eyes smiled at Bernice over the brim of her mug as she savoured her drink.

"Why, Sylvia Martin, are you suggesting my presence had something to do with causing these traumatic incidents?"

"No, just the opposite. For example, I remember forgetting to take my wallet to the grocery store and the humiliation of leaving all my selections at the cash. Then, as I was about to get in the car, weeping and empty-handed, you rolled up and dragged me back in to pay for my purchases."

"Ha! I'd forgotten that completely."

"You were my hero," said Sylvie.

"It worked both ways. Remember when we took the kids to the beach? Our boys playing happily in the water with their lifejackets on while we tanned and chatted. Then Josh fell forwards, face down in the water, and couldn't get back on his feet because of the lifejacket. You scooped him up in a blink. You saved his life that day." They clinked their mugs in a toast.

"I miss you."

"I miss you too, Sylvie my love. But Derek is doing so well since the transfer. I couldn't deny him the opportunity just because I miss my pal." Bernice scanned the crowded café. Small groups gathered at the petite round tables. Pairs of grey heads were interspersed among dreadlocks and pink hair. "This is a great town. Maybe Derek and I will come back when he retires."

"Speaking of Derek, I remember you crying when your children preferred the embrace of their father whenever they got injured."

"Oh, shit yes," Bernice laughed. "I was with them every minute of every day, wiping bottoms and mopping up vomit, but because he was an exotic, rare visitor, it was Derek they wanted."

"He's old school but a good man."

"I know. I remember my mother expressing amazement that any man would marry me." Bernice shook her head. "God, she was a judgmental old . . . but never mind the past. So, now that the kids are in school full-time, what do you do with your days?"

"Well, I decided to pursue some activities I always fantasized about."

"Tell me all about it." Bernice leaned forwards on her elbows.

"Do you remember how talented I was at art in high school?"

"Yes. You loved drawing and painting."

"Exactly," said Sylvie. "So, I signed up for two art classes. I'm going to take Beginner's Watercolour on Friday mornings at the Continuing Education Centre, and on Wednesday afternoons, there's a woman who teaches Zen Doodle Art in her home."

"What is Zen Doodle? Some kind of meditation?" asked Bernice.

"No, it's a pen and ink technique. A type of structured doodling, which is supposed to be relaxing. Hence the *Zen*."

"You used to doodle on everything in high school." Bernice traced a pattern on the table with her finger. "I remember your notebooks would be covered in shapes and words. Lots of psychedelic flowers and snippets of lyrics."

"Oh my, yes." Sylvie brushed a stray hair from her face. "And I used to get into such trouble for it. Now, teachers acknowledge that kids need to doodle to help them concentrate. Ha! Where was their understanding when I was in school?"

"I think it's brilliant that you're going to rediscover your creative side," said Bernice. "I expect to receive a framed doodle next Christmas."

"Sure thing."

"As for me . . . I have lots of volunteer commitments. I'm on the parent council at the kids' school. We organize fundraisers mostly, but it's a nice group of women, and I like the idea of contributing to the school community. I'm also involved in an environmental action committee."

Sylvie picked up her mug. "Oh? What's that about?"

"A water-bottling company wants to access the groundwater in our area. It's created a huge uproar because many people on the outskirts of town are still on private wells, the farms in particular, and people are worried the company will drain the aquifer," explained Bernice.

"I remember in college we were on the Green Team. Do you recall doing the campus tree inventory?"

"Yes."

"We had to measure and catalogue every single tree on campus. I remember some snotty engineering student saw me reaching around a tree to measure its circumference and he called me a—"

"Tree hugger," they said in unison, then laughed.

"He thought he was insulting me, but I remember being very proud of that," said Sylvie. She sat back in her chair and took a drink of her coffee. "Oh Bernie, will I ever find another friend who's as easy to talk to as you?"

"I think shared experience makes us so comfortable," said Bernice. "It'll take time to create another relationship as strong as ours. But here's the thing . . I'm not looking to replace you, Sylvie. Just because we're separated geographically doesn't mean we need to lose touch. Let's make a vow to video chat at least once a week. It costs nothing, and we can catch up on everything that's going on."

"Great idea."

"I'm going to lock myself in a closet and call you. I'll be able to whine and complain about Derek and the kids without them overhearing. Because whining is therapy. I really wouldn't change them for the world."

"We're both blessed," agreed Sylvie. "And who knows, maybe someday fate will bring you back here."

"Maybe."

"And it'll be like you never left."

Marion Reidel

Transformation

"So . . . how'd it go?" Denise held the mug handle in her right hand and propped her chin with her left. A clunky orange earring, almost the same shade as her lipstick, dangled from each lobe.

"It was transformational," said Sofia. "I could hardly wait to release Abby from her dated persona. It was well past time for her to present like a chic woman at least to the best of her ability. I amputated those childish curls." Sofia paused to drink her green tea.

Denise smiled. She'd anticipated hearing this story all week. Experience had taught her not to rush Sofia's narrative. She sat back and sipped her coffee, giving Sofia space to prepare her tale.

Five years ago, Sofia had come into Denise's vintage-clothing store and convinced her that she needed a retro style to match her merchandise. It was a turning point for her business and her social life. Now, Denise dressed like a cast member from *I Love Lucy*, and her customers considered her an icon of classic style.

"I cut her hair real short and perky. It's spiky and boyish like Ellen DeGeneres. No more Shirley Temple curls." Sofia laughed.

"Cute!"

"Then I gave Abby a makeup tutorial. I used the computer to match her skin tone, but I kept it light so her freckles would show through. Her skin is flawless." A conservatively dressed woman at the next table smiled and stroked her own cheek, possibly thinking that the comment was directed her way.

"Abby hates her freckles. How'd you get her to agree to that?" asked Denise.

Sofia snorted and took a drink of tea. "I don't ask for opinions or permission. I just tell my clients what's needed. Abby followed directions very nicely."

"They're funny things, freckles," said Denise. "They seem to go in and out of style. Celebrities like Lucy Liu and Emma Watson make freckles stylish. God, Morgan Freeman rocks some serious freckles."

"Exactly. Abby has perfect copper dots perched on her perfect cheekbones." Sofia laughed. "You know . . . I was at a trade show, and they were demonstrating temporary transfer freckles. You just rub them on like those kids' tattoos."

Denise laughed, too. "People will buy anything."

"And we always seem to want the opposite of what we have, eh? People with curly hair want straight. Those without freckles want them. Go figure." Sofia lifted the pot of green tea and refilled her mug. "I used charcoal liner to open her eyes and earthy shadows to accentuate the colour. She looks fabulous."

The woman at the next table smiled again, straightened the lapel of her suit jacket, and leaned towards Denise to catch more of their comments.

Denise loved Sofia's business, the Maven Day Spa. It offered a true escape from the world. From the moment a customer walked in, aromatherapy candles drew the stress from their pores, and ambient music transported them to another world. She also adored Sofia's partner, Fernando, who makes a delightful fuss over all the clients. Although she'd never been one to seek the spotlight, when Denise was at the spa, hidden from the world, she loved being pampered like a princess. Everything there felt luxurious: the marble floor, trayed ceiling, even the wall colour called Tranquil Waters. "It's sounds like business is going very well. You're a magician, Sofia."

"Business is going too well—that's the problem."

Denise laughed, then saw that her companion's facial expression was anything but humorous. "What d'you mean?"

"It sounds stupid, but there's more work than I can handle. I took on a junior stylist a couple of months ago, but we still can't keep up with the demand. Another beautician asked to join the team, but our space is just too small for a third workstation. My success is going to be my downfall because clients are getting pissed off at the lack of availability. My heads are going to competitors and directing them to reproduce my cuts. It's a disaster."

"Sounds like you need to expand your space."

"Exactly, and the tea shop next to me is moving to a new location, so I approached the landlord and asked if we could knock down the wall to expand the salon."

"Great. So, what's the problem?"

"Gee, Denise, can you loan me fifty thousand dollars for the renovation?"

"Fifty thousand dollars?"

"Yup. That's the quote I got for expanding the space, which includes buying three more chairs, mirrors, and a wash station. I don't have that kind of money."

"What about getting a bank loan?"

"I tried that. They laughed at me."

"Really? That's horrible."

The two women drank silently for several minutes. Each

pondered the irony of success threatening the viability of the business.

"What about crowdfunding?" asked Denise.

"What's that?"

"It's when you post on the internet that you need to raise money. You get a bunch of people to donate and offer a free haircut in return." Denise raised her eyebrows in what she imagined was a hopeful expression.

"My cuts cost between sixty and eighty dollars." Sofia pulled out her phone and tapped in a few numbers. "So I'd need to do over sixteen hundred cuts to pay people back. That would negate doing any paying work." Sofia waved her arms in frustration, striking the adjacent businesswoman still eavesdropping from the next table. "Oh shit. I'm sorry. Are you okay?" Sofia gushed.

"No worries," said the woman who turned more fully in Sofia's direction. "I don't mean to be rude or anything, but I couldn't help overhearing. It sounds like you operate a very interesting business."

"Sofia owns Maven Day Spa. She's the best stylist in town," said Denise. "Sofia creates powerful unique looks to bring out people's inner—"

"Release Your Inner Diva," Sofia said. "That's my slogan."

"And a wonderful concept it is," said the woman. "I'm totally serious when I say that both of you certainly exhibit distinct personal styles."

"I own Timeless, the vintage-clothing store downtown. That's how I met Sofia. Oh, I'm Denise by the way."

"This is a fortuitous moment for you. I'm Trudy Hardcastle."

"Hey Trud. Nice to meet you."

"It's Trudy." The woman pulled her chair over to their table. She extended her hand and gave Sofia's a firm shake. She handed them each a business card that was difficult to read due to its iridescent finish. "I own Rainbow Pooches Doggie Day Spa, a similar concept for our canine friends. Clearly you understand the power of one's inner self."

"The power of one's inner self . . . well said." Sofia's own wardrobe tended towards gothic romance. The majority of her attire was black with lace and velvet serving as key features on many items. Her hair was rich black with vibrant purple ends. A diamond stud sat in the crease of her nose, and her lobes were laden with multiple piercings. A colourful sleeve of tattoo art adorned her left arm. She said, "I think our bodies are a canvas for personal expression. Wearing mass-produced clothing indicates a lack of creativity."

"I couldn't agree more," said Trudy. "I don't mean to be funny, or anything, but what does my appearance tell you?"

Denise and Sophia carefully inspected the woman's light grey suit jacket and matching pants. There was a subtle weave pattern, and the pants had a sharp crease that held despite Trudy's crossed legs. Darts made the jacket hug her torso, denying any hint of masculinity. A fresh white shirt, unbuttoned to the collarbone, emphasized the jacket's colour. Simple pearl stud earrings were exposed by the upsweep of Trudy's mahogany hair.

"I think you look successful," said Denise.

"Seriously, what do you mean by that?" asked Trudy.

"Well, I don't know. You look tidy . . . businesslike."

"Your thoughts, Sophia?"

"Denise is right. You've got a well-crafted business style going on. You look very under control . . . like you're in charge . . . like you don't take crap from anyone."

"I just finished a very important meeting with an investor." Trudy crossed her legs in the other direction and leaned in to the table. "I think it should be obvious this outfit is a uniform to convince the men I do business with to take me seriously. It sends them a message. It says I'm competent, and they react appropriately."

"Unlike the bankers who brushed me off," said Sofia.

"Exactly. I'm not being funny when I tell you to think of your wardrobe as a series of costumes. You have your edgy work persona, maybe a fun casual style on the weekend, probably a sexy hot mama outfit for going out at night . . ."

"You're right on that account." Denise giggled. "You should see how men react to Sofia's red-leather dress."

"It has drool stains on the shoulder." The women laughed.

"And it's not just clothing as you know. It's makeup, hair, the whole image, right?"

"Of course. That's the whole premise of my business." Sofia felt as if she was stepping into a trap.

"And . . . powerful body language, good vocabulary, and prepared documentation are also necessary factors to secure corporate attention." Trudy paused to see whether her companions were following. "I've been a successful business owner for a long time, and it's my experience that bankers, male or female, do not respond well to women who express creativity through attire, but they do sit up and pay attention to anyone who looks traditionally businesslike."

Sophia and Denise looked at each other.

"I'm a powerful mentor. Perhaps you'd like *me* to transform *you* into a powerful businesswoman before you schedule another conversation with a financial backer. I find that a meticulous spreadsheet, combined with a well-tailored suit and a pair of high heels, opens a lot of doors."

"Like preparing for a performance," said Sofia.

"Putting your game face on," said Trudy.

Drinks with Mother

Negativity emanated from my mother like the glow of a light bulb. Although I'd made progress cutting back my coffee consumption, sitting with her, I was on my third mug.

"Yesterday's supper was Beef-O-Juice. I've chewed shoe leather that was more tender."

"Really, Mom? You chewed shoe leather?"

"It's just a saying, Sandra." My mother scowled. "I tell you the meals are inedible. The other day, the dessert, called Peaches à la Cream, was just canned peaches with Cool Whip on top. A fancy name doesn't make the dessert any better. The food is atrocious, and the portions are meager." She took a sip of her tea then picked up her fork. "I've eaten better hospital food, and yes, Sandra, I have eaten hospital food."

My mother lives in a facility that claims to offer a gracious retirement lifestyle. She has a one-bedroom apartment that is larger than my first marital home. Meals are offered in a communal dining room. When grocery shopping, I often fantasize about wandering to a dining hall for meals. No planning, no prep, no cleanup, no complaints. Nothing I cook appeals to my son and daughter.

"How's the cheesecake, Mom?"

"It's extremely dry, and the cherry topping is more goo than cherries."

I take her out every weekend to give the staff a break as much as to offer a change of scenery for her. "I think you're lucky that someone makes all your meals." I spoke in a practiced cheery tone. "Cooking for your grandkids is frustrating. Devon only likes sugary cereal and pizza, while Amber is constantly on some fad diet with incomprehensible rules." I smiled as I reached over to shift my mother's folded walker so the couple at the next table could depart.

"At that age, you either ate everything I put in front of you or you got nothing at all. You spoil those kids."

Domestic skills are not my strong point. Like many single parents, I find that after work, I'm exhausted. I microwave a low-calorie dinner for one, pour a glass of red wine, and light a candle to pretend I'm dining. It took determination not to take her bait.

The café was filled with people engaged in pleasant conversation, embellished with sprinkles of laughter. I estimated that my mother would need five minutes to finish her dessert.

"Sandra, are you listening?" I had drifted to interior monologue and failed to acknowledge my mother's moaning on cue.

"I beg your pardon. What did you say?"

"That new woman. No one wants to eat with her."

"Why not?"

"Her table manners are awful." My mother spoke as she popped a forkful of cheesecake into her mouth. "She eats with her fingers. Her hands are so arthritic she can't hold her cutlery, and so she picks up everything with her fingers—her meat, her lettuce . . . It's awful. I told her they'll cut her food in the kitchen, but she doesn't want to be a bother. I guess it's better that we should suffer." She took another bite of dessert and continued without swallowing. "She chews with her mouth open. Watching her is enough to make you sick."

My mother blustered between bites of cheesecake and sips of tea. A morsel of crumble crust nestled in the corner of her mouth, a faint stain rested over her left breast on her shirt, and when she spoke, she spat.

"I tell you the place is turning into a loony bin. There are so many walkers lined up in the hallway you can hardly get past them at dinnertime."

"But Mom, you use a walker."

"Now, they let in a woman who's blind. She has dark glasses and a cane."

"She may've been blind all her life. You might discover she's perfectly capable."

"It's not gracious retirement living, Sandra. It's a nut house. Last week that Italian woman . . ."

I'd heard the story multiple times. A guest performer visits, and that lady requests an Italian song no matter what the performer's genre. Celtic guitarists, Country and Western Duos, the choir from the local elementary school, all get the same request. Personally, I think it's hilarious.

" . . . and her granddaughter only stayed for an hour. Not much of a visit if you ask me. Did I tell you about Gloria?"

"Yes, you did. She's in the hospital due to back problems."

"She has disintegrating discs. It's very painful, and there's nothing . . ."

My mother had been repeating stories for years. I used to be able to deflect a repeat performance by demonstrating possession of the information being offered, but this no longer works. Once the story is cued up, it cannot be stopped. I do feel sorry for Gloria. Back problems are awful.

As my mother's monologue continued, I listened to pace rather than content. At pauses, I nodded to suggest attentiveness while being blissfully adrift in my own thoughts. While I semilistened, I looked out the plate glass window behind her. The sun had set, and streetlights lit the heritage streetscape beautifully.

I'm sure mom's "fellow inmates," as she calls them, think I'm an only child. My brother chooses not to participate in eldercare issues. He spends hours in arenas, feeding his son's misguided dream of hockey stardom. I read an article somewhere that Canadian kids have a four-thousand-to-one chance of making it into the NHL. When I get depressed about Devon's lack of initiative, I comfort myself with the fact that he's not chasing unrealistic aspirations.

" . . . and then he clobbered him with his cane," announced my mother.

"He what?"

"He hit him over the head with his cane," she repeated.

"I'm sorry, Mom. I lost track of the story. Who hit whom?"

"That three-hundred-pound man, the one they needed to order a special dining room chair for. He hit Bert over the head. Bert had to go to the hospital. He got five staples in his head."

"Why would the man hit Bert with his cane?" She had me now.

"The big man asked Bert why his wife hadn't come down for dinner. Bert said she was stuck in her power lift chair. Apparently she can't figure out how to use the controls. Bert got tired of helping her, so he said she could sit there until she figured it out, and he came down to dinner without her."

"That's mean."

"The big man thought so, too. He called Bert an ass and hit him over the head with his cane. Bert had to go to the hospital and get fifteen staples."

"What about the wife? Did anyone go and rescue her?" I asked.

"I don't know, but that three-hundred-pound galoot was told to stay in his room. They're sending his meals up to him."

"What about Bert? Did anyone speak to him about helping his

wife?"

"I don't know, Sandra. That's not the point of the story. The point is that Bert has fifty staples in his head because the place is a loony bin." My mother drank the end of her tea. "This tea is cold. Let's get out of this place."

"I'm not finished my pie."

"Pie is the last thing you need. You put on a lot of weight since your divorce. You're never going to find another man looking like that."

I took a deep breath to absorb the sting of this psychic slap. "Thanks for your concern, Mother."

As I went through the ritual of setting up her walker and helping her on with her coat, I felt acutely aware of people watching. Sometimes I feel their judgment, other times empathy.

"Ouch. You bumped my sore shoulder. I need the top button done. I can't reach my purse. It goes on this side. You're blocking my way." She executes a series of statements rather than requests.

I guided her through the tables, offering apologies to patrons as we bumped past them. A woman my age held the door for us and whispered, "You're doing a great job," as I passed. I almost burst into tears at this small act of kindness.

I loaded my mother and her apparatus into my car and returned her to the retirement home she likes to call "that place you put me in." My obligation fulfilled, I headed home to eat my low-calorie microwave dinner, drink a glass of red wine, and light a candle.

Marion Reidel

On the Contra

"You took up square dancing?"

"No! Let go of the stereotype." Kris was offended by Denise's accusation. "You're thinking of 1950s hoedowns. I mean, I know you love vintage clothing, but some of us are living in the present." Kris laughed to suggest her comment was not a criticism. She scrambled to get her friend onside. "By the way, I really like that top. I noticed it the last time you wore it."

Denise looked at her own chest. "Oh this? It's an authentic peasant blouse. Hand-embroidered in Chile. They're imported by a Christian mission organization. Cost me ten bucks each. I sell 'em for eighty dollars."

"Nice profit." Kris thought the blouse looked like something a hippie would wear. At least Denise didn't have bare shoulders. "Hey, didn't you take dance lessons as a kid?"

"Mmm. Yeah. Not by choice." Denise replied with a mouth full of brownie. "My mother made me take Highland dancing. Only daughter syndrome."

"Well, you might enjoy contra dancing. It's not competitive." Kris sipped her coffee.

"Dancing in lines and linking arms with partners. Sounds like square dancing with a new name. Yee-haw and all that, right?"

"No. First of all, there's a group of musicians, not just a fiddler. And the music is much more contemporary."

"Really?" Denise smirked. "Are there cowboy hats, tight jeans, and pointy-toed boots? Like the stuff they do at the Golden Corral on Thursday nights?"

"No. That's country line dancing." Kris raised her voice unintentionally. She took a measured breath and continued, "Contra does not use country and western music, either. We don't wear those crinoline dresses with gingham that matches a partner's shirt. There are no cowboy hats or boots. Most people wear comfortable shoes, T-shirts and shorts or maybe a flowy skirt. You'd like that."

"Hmm."

"Personally, I like the way a long skirt swirls when I turn," said Kris, hoping to trigger her friend's passion for vintage fashion.

"Right." Denise ate the last bite of her brownie.

"It's fun. If you gave it a try, you'd enjoy it."

Denise licked her fingertips. "Having someone call out the steps sounds a little too much like gym class to me. Remember Miss Battersby in her powder-blue velour tracksuit? She always had a whistle around her neck and a hair growing out of her chin." Denise laughed and took a drink of tea.

"You're such a snob. The benefit of having a caller is so that anyone can join in. They tells us the moves as we go, so everyone can follow along. It's fun, honestly."

"I remember 'Turkey in the Straw' and 'The Grand Old Duke of York' from grade ten girls' phys. ed. It was a nightmare." Denise sang,

The Grand Old Duke of York,
He had ten thousand men;
He marched them to the top of the hill,
And he marched them down again.

"Would you rather stay home and watch decorating shows on a Friday night?" Kris held eye contact with her long-time friend and waited.

Denise continued,

> And when they were up, they were up,
> And when they were down, they were down,
> And when they were only halfway up,
> They were neither up nor down.

"Don't judge, Kris. Just because you PVR the Friday night shows doesn't make you any less addicted." Denise smirked.

An uncomfortable silence wrapped around their table. The women had met during high school. Now, Denise ran a successful vintage clothing store, and Kris operated a daycare centre. They'd been lucky in business—but unlucky in love, supporting each other through a series of failed relationships. Denise's most recent ended after five years because her boyfriend didn't grow out of not wanting children, but instead, became more entrenched in their self-focused double-income-no-kids lifestyle.

"You need to get back in the game," had been Kris's advice. They were both approaching thirty, and the ticking of their biological timepieces was becoming downright intrusive. At work each day, Kris's heart was tugged by her young charges. She felt sure her friend must sense her desperation. "Your prime reproductive years are limited."

"Don't remind me."

"I'm just saying what must be said, Denise. We can't waste more time sitting home on our own. We need to get out and socialize." Kris's mug sat empty, but she didn't want to break momentum by getting a refill.

"Listen, I'm glad you're having fun. I just don't think I'd fit in."

"What are you talking about? It's a real mixed group. There's everyone from families with kids to senior citizens. It's even an LGBTQ-friendly crowd. Honestly, it's tons of fun."

Denise sighed. "I'm not really looking for a family-friendly Friday night. Socializing with seniors is *not* on my list, and LGBTQ folks don't qualify as my target market." She smiled weakly. "If you want an outing, why don't we go to a bar and meet some eligible men?"

"Denise." Kris smiled. "At contra dancing, everyone dances with everyone else. There *are* eligible men . . . and women are free to make the first invitation." Kris's problem was that the man she had her sights on came with a buddy. Denise was the answer to peeling away that barrier.

"Really? What's the ratio of desperate women to eligible men?"

"Stop it. It's not like that at all. And get this . . .contra dancers are supposed to make eye contact with each partner. It enhances the connectivity of the experience. They say it even helps reduce dizziness when being swung around." Kris laughed. "When I first joined, one guy swung me so hard I ended up on my ass. It was hilarious."

"Hilarious is not what I'm looking for."

"Well, let me ask you this . . . where else can you have a different partner thrust into your arms every thirty seconds?"

"Seriously, Kris, what kind of men?" Denise touched her empty plate.

"Okay. Well, one guy is a carpenter, another owns his own electrical business, one is a dairy farmer—"

"A farmer?" Denise gave her whole body a pronounced shudder.

"Honey, I'm talking about a farm with over five hundred cows.

It's more like running a factory than old-school farming." Kris reached across the table and poked her friend in the shoulder. "The members come from all kinds of backgrounds. There's a computer geek and an actuary if you prefer. These are mature men, not foolish boys, and they're fit."

Denise shook her head and took a drink of her tea.

"Picture this . . ." Kris began gesturing. "The gym lights are lowered to create the sense of an anonymous large space. It could be a ballroom in a French chateau or a Scottish manor house. The crowd has gathered for some festival, perhaps a pagan harvest celebration or in honour of visiting nobility. The melodies might be ancient, surviving from seventeenth-century England, or they could be an Appalachian adaptation of African rhythms. In either case, the tempo sweeps through the crowd. The voice of the caller leads the way. There's a whirl of fabric, and body temperatures rise as dancers move through the figures, passing from partner to partner. Your eyes meet a series of returning gazes. Strong masculine features reaching out to you both literally, as you are swept into muscular arms, and spiritually as they connect with your soul. You're transported, by music and movement, into another world. A gracious past where women were honoured and men were strong. Eventually, moving without conscious thought, you trace the prescribed formation, merging with your fellow dancers to create a living work of art. You're a speck of paint on canvas, a note wafting from an instrument, a—"

"Give it a rest." Denise couldn't help but laugh. "You sound like you're reading advertising copy. What you're really talking about is a bunch of left-footed locals in the high school gym being directed around like school children."

"Well . . ." Kris felt her body deflate.

"What time are you picking me up?"

Marion Reidel

An Epidemic

"An epidemic is spreading through Canadian culture." Jeremy enjoys pontificating. His comments are directed beyond his companion to anyone who might overhear. "The problem is not limited to a specific age, economic, or ethnic group. As with most major illnesses, the cause is a mixture of genetic and environmental factors." He taps his phone to see whether he missed any texts.

"The symptoms of this disease are easily identified, and the cure is simple." He adds a pause for dramatic effect. "I call the disease . . . Oblivieitis." Jeremy smirks at his own wit. His companion's brows rise in interest. Jeremy takes a sip of his latte to sustain the suspense.

"This disease renders people unaware of those around them." He continues, voice slightly raised to compensate for the chatter at the next table. "Infected individuals, perceiving themselves as central in this universe, become unable to evaluate their impact on others. No treatment is sought because they're unable to recognize the infection."

His companion smiles. The cleverness of the medical metaphor is understood. Someday, Jeremy hopes to find a global audience for his insights.

"Oblivieitis symptoms are easily identified. Let me give you an example." He taps his fingertips in a steeple, then begins to gesture as he speaks. "A couple strolling along the sidewalk approaches a group heading in the opposite direction engaged in animated conversation. The couple moves to single file as the moment of meeting nears, but the Oblivieitis victims continue in a cluster, forcing them to step completely off the sidewalk." Jeremy makes a sweeping gesture with his left arm and strikes one of the café's servers.

His companion's snort of acknowledgment, or amusement, fuels Jeremy to continue. "Or how about this . . ." His manner becomes more animated. "A retail employee stands outside a store, having a smoke at an appropriate distance from the entrance. They take a last draw on their cigarette and then just toss it to the ground, stamp it out, and walk inside, having added to the minefield of butts outside their place of business." He makes an exaggerated gesture of incredulity and scans the café noting several returned glances.

Taking his last bite of cookie, Jeremy continues while still chewing. "Texting pedestrians cross intersections without looking. Cyclists wearing headphones speed through traffic. Coffee shop patrons place orders without noticing the line." He nods to indicate the café's counter.

Jeremy sets his empty plate on the next table to create space to lean forwards on his elbows. "People in cafés converse in loud voices. Fast food patrons don't clear their debris. Grocery store shoppers leave their cart in the middle of the aisle. Drivers back out of parking spaces without looking or ignore signs and park inappropriately in specially designated locations." Jeremy takes another drink of his latté and leans back.

His companion leans in, awaiting the sermon's conclusion.

"Parents ignore their screaming child. Dog owners carry a leash while their beloved pet runs free to sniff people's private parts.

Clerks socialize with colleagues while customers wait in line. Passengers put their bags on crowded transit seats while I stand. Cars merge without signalling. People unwrap crinkly candies at the theatre. The lack of social awareness is astonishing!" Jeremy emphasizes his point with a slam of his palm on the table. There's a notable pause in conversation throughout the room that he interprets as curiosity.

"The cure costs nothing and is readily available," he says with a wag of his finger. "The name of the antidote varies, but the ingredients are essentially the same." Another pause is injected. He leans forwards and locks eyes with his companion. "Whether you call it courtesy, awareness, mindfulness, or respect, all that is needed is a realization that our actions impact others, the environment, and ourselves." With one final emphatic gesture, Jeremy knocks over the remainder of his latte and watches as the pool of creamy coffee rains on the carpet.

Marion Reidel

The Diagnosis

"I figured out what's wrong with me." Marg interrupted her friends' conversation as she joined them at the café's front window and set down her tea.

"Ha! There's nothing wrong with you." Annie patted the back of Marg's liver-spotted hand.

"You're Superwoman." Dorothy smirked, knowing it was exactly what her friend wanted to hear, then she gave two sugar packets a shake, tore them open, and dumped them into her empty cup. "What are you gals planning to bring to the church potluck?"

"I saw a documentary with that Oprah doctor," Marg stated.

"I know the one. He's so handsome." Annie smiled. "What's his name?"

Waving her spoon, Marg said, "That's not important. The thing is—"

"Dr. Oz," offered Dorothy. "I always remember his name."

"How?" asked Annie.

"Well . . . I'm Dorothy, like in *The Wizard of Oz*. Associations help me remember."

The women chuckled. The elderly trio met weekly at this café to tend to their friendship. They'd been patrons for almost a decade and preferred the table for three at the window.

"That's funny," said Annie. "When I associate things, I just get them more mixed up. For example"—she added two creams to her coffee—"that contractor Peter and I hired to redo our bathroom—"

"Oh, your renovation turned out so well," said Dorothy. "I love the tile you chose."

"Thanks. Turquoise is my favourite colour."

Marg pulled air in between her teeth.

Dorothy cast her a quick frown and turned back to Annie. "You were telling us about your contractor."

"What? Oh, right. He had the same name as Peter's brother. I kept calling the man Frank, but that was the wrong brother." Annie laughed.

"Isn't the other brother named Harvey?" asked Dorothy. "Was the contractor Harvey Breckmann? He did Elise Watkins's kitchen reno. Have you seen it? White country-style cabinets with Montclair Danby crosscut marble counters. They have a beautiful deep green vein which coordinates with the glass-tile backsplash—"

"Hey, I was trying to explain how I figured out what's wrong with me. Isn't that more important than Elise Watkins's kitchen?"

"Sorry, Marg. We're all ears. How did Dr. Oz help you?" asked Dorothy. She lifted the lid on her teapot, releasing a sweet floral aroma. The trio's friendship spanned thirty years. Dorothy had learned that Marg believed her opinions to be of utmost interest to everyone.

"Well, I'm glad you asked. This information might be helpful to both of you." Observing that Dorothy's tea was ready, Marg lifted her own pot. "It was a very interesting show about a new illness called Adult Onset ADD." She poured her tea, dribbling in the process. "Darn this teapot. The yellow one was taken." Marg wiped the table with a disposable napkin. "He went through all the symptoms, and that's what's wrong with me."

Annie took a bite of her oatmeal cookie, then covered her mouth with her hand. "What symptoms?"

Marg took Annie's napkin to absorb the puddle in her saucer. "Well, the biggest one is forgetting things."

"We all forget things." Dorothy tried to decide whether to take those yummy frozen phyllo appetizers or a tray of crackers and cheese to the potluck on Sunday.

"Andrea tells me that I repeat stories," said Annie. "I think I have something new to share with her, and she interrupts me and says, 'Mom, you already told me that.' It's a mystery."

"That's what I'm talking about." Marg leaned in, insistent.

"The other day, I couldn't remember the name of that actor. The one who played James Bond," said Annie.

"Roger Moore. He was a dream." Placing the back of her hand to her forehead, Dorothy rolled back her eyes in a mock swoon.

"No, the other one. The one with the beautiful accent," said Annie.

"Oh, Pierce Brosnan." Dorothy sighed. "He sounds so classy."

"No, no, the other one. The one from Scotland."

"Oh, I know who you mean. He was in a medieval movie, *Robin Hood* or *King Arthur*." Dorothy snapped her fingers. "His name is on the tip of my tongue."

"Yes, that's the guy. He played the captain of a Russian submarine and Harrison Ford's father in the *Indiana Jones* movie. What's his darn name?" Exasperated, Annie tapped her temple with her index finger.

"I can hear him now. A smooth Scottish accent." Dorothy lowered her voice and mimed holding a cigarette to her lips. "My name's Bond, James Bond."

"Is he still alive?" asked Annie.

"I think so," replied Dorothy. "Don't you hate how men become chiselled with age, while our bodies erode?" The two women laughed and sipped their hot drinks.

"Sean Connery," muttered Marg.

"What?" asked Annie.

"The actor's name. It's Sean Connery." Marg sipped her tea, giving her companions a stern expression over the mug's edge.

"There's nothing wrong with your memory," said Annie. "I've been trying to recall his name all week."

"Yes, there is something wrong. If you two would focus for a minute, I'll explain what I found out." Marg's tone sounded more like a reprimand than she intended. She paused, smiled, and then added, "You might find it interesting."

Dorothy nodded. "I'm sure we will. You have our complete attention. Go ahead." She liked the assortment of frozen Asian appetizers from the bulk store, but the grocery store brand was cheaper.

"Thank you. So, ADD stands for Attention Deficit Disorder. It usually happens in children. They're restless and can't pay attention in school. Sometimes they even need medication."

"Like Audrey's grandson," said Dorothy. "I ran into her at the library on Saturday, and she had little Joey in tow."

"Oh, that reminds me, I need to return a book. I never did finish it. I need to write these things down." Annie started rummaging through her purse.

"Audrey and I stopped to chat for five minutes, and the child couldn't be still. He pulled her skirt and touched the book display. When he started yanking magazines out of the rack, Audrey said she had to go, and she dragged him screaming out the door."

"Oh dear." Annie set her purse back down. "How embarrassing."

"Exactly," said Marg. "Lots of kids are distractible, and Dr. Oz said the same thing can happen to adults. That's why he calls it Adult Onset ADD."

The three women took synchronized sips.

Marg continued. "Have you ever walked into a room and forgotten why you went there?"

"Yes."

"Or have you gone to the store and couldn't remember what you needed to buy?"

"I make a list," said Annie.

"Do you misplace your keys?"

"Yes."

"And retell stories?"

Dorothy could tell Marg was enjoying the spotlight.

"Or forget words, especially people's names?"

"Sure, once I—"

"These are symptoms of Adult Onset ADD."

"I thought it was just old age." Annie giggled.

"Doesn't everyone suffer from memory problems?" asked Dorothy. She wondered whether she had a coupon for the bulk food store.

"Apparently not," replied Marg. She took another sip. "And, memory problems lead to bigger issues."

"Like what?" asked Annie.

"Like getting lost," suggested Dorothy. "I heard Charlie Watson went for a walk last week and got so turned around he couldn't find his house. He was wandering the neighbourhood for two hours until his dog got hungry and dragged him home."

"Dogs can be very smart," said Annie. "I heard once about a dog who could find people buried in an avalanche. It could hear them, or smell them, or something."

"June said Charlie had a real scare. He thought he was losing his mind. Imagine getting lost in your own neighbourhood."

Dorothy shook her head and sipped her tea.

"Ladies!" Marg, fingers tightly entwined, set her hands on the edge of the table. "That's what I'm talking about. Dr. Oz says adults with ADD miss appointments and are late for work. They're forgetful and distracted. They cause more car accidents. It's easy for them to get delayed or lost. This is a serious matter."

"I make lists. I use a datebook that fits into my purse, and I write everything down." Annie lifted her purse from its position at her feet and set it on the table. She proudly withdrew a small blue book and held it open for her companions to see. "Each page is a week," she explained. "I write in my appointments and a to-do list. See here? On today's page, it says coffee with Marg and Dorothy, Conversation Café, three o'clock. And here I am." She smiled triumphantly.

"Well done," said Dorothy. "Oh, you're getting a pedicure on Thursday? Are you going to Almost Heaven?"

"No. I got a coupon for the new place in the mall." Annie indicated the slip attached to the calendar page. "It's one of those jazzy places with fancy massage chairs and bubbling foot baths."

"Sounds nice," said Dorothy. "Going to get your usual pink?"

"Something more tropical, I think. Perhaps a nice turquoise."

"Honestly, you two are killing me." Marg sat back with arms crossed.

"What's the matter?" asked Annie.

"What's the matter?" Marg ran her fingers through her curly salt-and-pepper hair. "What's the matter? I'll tell you what's the matter. I'm trying to share some important information, and you two cannot stay on topic for a minute."

"Maybe we're suffering from ADD." Dorothy smirked and sipped her tea.

"Maybe you are," Marg shot back. "And so maybe it's even more important that you hear this information."

Dorothy made a gesture of zipping her lips. Annie picked up her coffee mug and said, "You go right ahead, sweetie."

"It's one thing to get lost walking a dog," explained Marg. "Driving a car is even more dangerous. People with ADD become confused. They panic and try to make a turn they missed, or change lanes without looking, and the next thing you know, they caused an accident. Being a distracted driver is not just about kids using cellphones. Seniors, like us, can be just as distracted by the confusion within our minds."

"Worrisome." Annie finished her cookie, searched for her napkin, then wiped crumbs from the corners of her mouth with the back of her hand.

"Like when Wilbur Barnstable ran into the back of a firetruck . . ." Dorothy began before catching herself and repeating the zipped-lip signal.

"Yes, just like Wilbur Barnstable," agreed Marg. "I mean, for goodness sake. The truck was parked at the side of the road with flashing lights all over it. He's lucky he didn't kill a firefighter."

"I remember that," said Annie. "Midtown Shoes had a fire in the basement. Bad wiring or something. The next week they had a smoke and water damage sale. Everything less than fifty percent."

"I heard they still made a profit because the insurance paid for the spoiled stock and they sold it, too," said Dorothy. "Elise Watkins bought four pairs of dress shoes in specific colours to match—"

"To heck with Elise Watkins!" Marg glanced around then lowered her voice to a harsh whisper. "Honest to goodness, you two are a trial. We're talking about a serious illness that I'm suffering from. You two admitted you're experiencing memory loss. Clearly you're easily distracted. We need to be aware of this before it disrupts our lives and our relationships."

The women sat in silence for a moment as the chatter of the

café's patrons surrounded them. In a subdued voice, Marg continued, "Dr. Oz says doing crosswords and so-day-koo can—"

"Sue-doh-ku," said Dorothy.

"What?"

"You pronounced it incorrectly. It's sue-doh-ku."

"What's the difference how the word is said, Dorothy? You're completely missing my point. You know I'm talking about those stupid number puzzles. There's no need to correct me. The point is, if we don't exercise our brains, we'll suffer memory loss and the inability to focus. This is something you need to be worried about because problems escalate. Dr. Oz said the lack of focus leads to impatience because your mind can't settle. Then this leads to quick tempers, which can be very trying for those around you. It's a serious disorder." Marg exhaled and slumped back in her chair.

"Impatience you say?" asked Annie.

"And quick tempers," said Dorothy. "I can see how that would put a strain on relationships."

The three women finished their drinks and snacks in silence.

Useful Information

"This place is friggin' expensive."

"Don't worry, Toby. I'm paying. How do you take your coffee?"

"Double cream and four sugars."

"Why don't you find a seat?"

Jennifer watched Toby's black-clad figure shuffle past available tables. He tucked himself into a corner.

"Afternoon, Jenn. Regular order? Mountain Hagen organic, black, right? That an internet date you have there?"

"Very funny, Marcia. And a medium Americano with two cream and two sugars."

"You taking a break from the kids? This isn't your regular time."

"Doing a favour for a high school classmate. Her brother needs to find a job."

"Any excuse to talk to other adults, eh?" Both women laughed.

Jennifer hiked up her overstuffed shoulder bag, and carried the drinks to the table. "Here you go, Toby."

"Um. Cool. Thanks." Toby took the mug and slumped back.

"So, your sister tells me you're looking for work."

"Yeah. Sure. Cool." Toby ran his index finger over the table's scarred surface.

"I'm a stay-at-home mom now, but I used to work in HR. It's hard to find employment." Jennifer took a drink. Toby's ball cap and hoodie combo presented a definite adolescent vibe. He seemed younger than his twenty-two years.

"I know your sister from high school. Hadn't seen her in . . . years. Then we bumped into each other at the mall last week. When she asked if I'd help you, I thought it would be a good chance for me to keep my skills up."

Toby grunted acknowledgment.

"I plan to return to Consolidated Fabricating. They manufacture car parts . . . air conditioning components and security alarms, mostly. I've been off for almost two years. I have two girls. Amy's eighteen months, and Rosie's three months."

Toby continued to trace the table's texture.

"Thank goodness Rosie still naps." She took another sip. "Do you *want* to find a job?"

"Yeah. Sure. Cool."

Jennifer noticed an elderly lady at the next table complaining about her teapot.

"I understand you don't have much expericnce."

"Yeah. No."

"Tell me about your job history."

"Cool. Sure." Toby scratched his nose and looked up at the ceiling. "My first job was a paper route."

"Okay." Jennifer dug her pen and journal out of her shoulder bag.

"Mom usually did it."

"Oh. Well, what else have you done?"

"I worked at McDonald's."

"Good. Employers know a kid trained by McDonald's will demonstrate a solid work ethic." She opened her book and clicked the pen. "How long did you work there?"

"Ah. Eleven days, I think. Yeah. Eleven."

"Eleven days?" Her pen hovered. "What happened?"

"They didn't like when I used the floor mop to wipe table tops. Stupid rule. It was faster." Toby took a drink and then tilted up the visor of his hat. "I worked at a gas station last summer."

"Tell me about that." Jennifer smiled, pen poised.

"I worked nights. People bought gas, or smokes, or snacks. I got held up once."

She wrote *customer service*. "Really? How did you handle it?"

"I gave 'em what they wanted. Shit, I don't wanna die because some shithead wants smokes."

One of the adjacent elderly ladies scowled at Toby. Jennifer leaned forwards and whispered, "Can you avoid using swear words?"

"Oh, shit! Sorry. Yeah." Toby sat up.

"So, you were telling me about the job at the gas station."

"My uncle was pissed."

"Your uncle?"

"He owned the gas station. He was mad because the guy took six cartons of smokes. He says to me, 'That's over two hundred dollars. I'm gonna take that outta your pay.' An' I say, 'My life's worth more than frickin' two hundred dollars, so you can shove your job up your . . .' ah, 'butt.'"

"So, you were fired?"

"Hell, no. Mom wouldn't let him fire me. He laid me off."

Jennifer raised her eyebrows. "Do you think he would serve as your reference?"

Toby tilted his head and curled his lip. "What?"

"Would he say complimentary things about you if a potential employer called?"

"Yeah . . . No."

"That's unfortunate." They broke eye contact to drink. Jennifer looked up. "Would he help if your mom asked him to?"

"They don't talk anymore."

Jennifer rested her forehead in her palm. Toby drank.

The old ladies rose and gathered their belongings. As they shuffled past, one inadvertently dropped a purple kerchief. Toby plucked it from the floor and called after the departing trio. "Hey, lady, you dropped something." He rose and handed the kerchief to her.

Jennifer heard the old woman mumble a begrudging thank you. She underlined *customer service*. When Toby was reseated, she said, "Okay . . . are there other jobs I should hear about?"

"I worked at the Salvation Army Store."

"What did you do there?"

"Whatever they told me to. Swept the floor, threw out stuff, put crap back on shelves." Toby adjusted his ball cap to be exactly straight. "Ya know, people take things, then decide they don't want it, and just put it anywhere. It's . . . like . . . a full-time job just putting crap back."

"Well, in HR we call that merchandise handling and routine maintenance." Jennifer made a note while Toby drank his coffee. "Dare I ask how long you worked there?"

"Fifty hours."

"Hours? Was it a volunteer position?"

"No. The court said I had to work there because I got caught with weed. It was total crap." Toby drained his coffee.

Jennifer put down her pen and sat back. "Toby, we've got a problem. You see, a resumé is the basic tool for seeking employment. None of your experience is suitable for listing."

"Yeah. Shit." Toby lowered his head.

Jennifer doodled as she fantasized about ways she could be spending her free afternoon. Getting a much-needed manicure, cleaning the oven, rewatching the Marie Kondo video on how to fold underwear.

"Gee. Crap." Toby began chewing the nails of his left hand.

"It's okay." Jennifer picked up her pen and straightened her book. "Let's approach this like you're looking for your first job. Instead of listing experience, we'll focus on your abilities and interests. Things you're good at. Things you like to do. We'll massage them into work-related skills. That will help us identify what sort of job you like to do. Does that make sense?"

"Yeah. Cool. Sure."

"Great." Jennifer prepared to write. "So, what are you good at?"

"Gaming."

"Gaming?"

"Yeah. Right. Cool."

"Can you be more specific? What does gaming involve?" She began writing.

"I go on quests. Get skills and find stuff . . . for points. I've got a tribe of eight hundred and they help me fight. I've got weapons and special skills. Ya know, supernatural stuff like going invisible and seeing through walls. It's tough 'cuz you gotta remember where everything is, ya know, what way you went and what's behind doors. You only get so many lives, so ya can't afford to mess up."

Jennifer looked up.

"I'm fast, and I can leap real high." Toby tried to take a drink, but realized his mug was empty. "There's a buncha guys that I play with online. They're beginners. They always ask what to do."

"Do you play this game a lot?"

"'Bout five hours."

"A week?"

"A day. On the weekends it's 'bout, I guess, twelve."

"Twelve hours!"

"Yeah. Sure."

"No wonder you haven't got a job." Jennifer laughed. Toby seemed confused. "Okay, here's what we can say. You have excellent task focus. You don't mind repetitive tasks. Your fine motor control is strong. You learn quickly, and your visual memory is excellent. You're motivated by achievement, learn from mistakes, and cooperate with co-workers. In fact, you showed leadership in orienting newcomers." Jennifer felt her heartbeat increase.

"Yeah. That's cool." Toby lifted his empty mug.

"Would you like another coffee, Toby?"

"Yeah. No. That's okay."

"You sure?"

"Yeah. No."

"Okay. We're making progress. What else are you good at?"

"Lemme think." Toby lifted the brim of his hat and rubbed his forehead, causing the hood of his sweater to fall back.

"Hey, Toby."

"Yeah?"

"Let's talk about how you're dressed for a minute."

"Huh?"

"What's with the hat?"

"Ya like it? Cool."

"Well, Toby, I think if you went to a job interview wearing a hat that says Bitch Relax on it, the interviewer would find it offensive."

"Yeah?"

"Yes. Especially if you're being interviewed by a woman."

Toby removed his hat to inspect the embroidered words. "It's like . . . a brand."

"That's fine for your personal life, but, I think, in a work place, you shouldn't wear clothing that people find offensive."

"It's just saying relax. Some bitches, I mean... . . . um . . .

women are all up in your face. Ya know?"

"I'm giving you helpful advice. Don't wear that hat. No—don't wear any hat to a job interview. Got it? No hats."

"Yeah. No. Cool."

"While we're on the topic, let's talk about your hoodie. I know that Thug Life is a clothing line, but . . . the reference suggests . . . I don't know . . . some level of criminal activity."

"Gangs. Yeah."

"Gangs are fun and cool in music videos, but employers don't want to hire someone who glamorizes criminal activity. Do you understand what I'm saying?"

"No hoodie. Yeah. Cool."

Jennifer could see Toby was fading. "Let's get back to your talents. What else are you good at? What other special skills do you have?"

Toby sighed and played with his empty mug.

Jennifer waited.

"I speak Dothraki." He had a hopeful expression.

"I beg your pardon? I'm not familiar with that."

"It's from *Game of Thrones*. It's the warrior language of Khal Drogo's tribe."

"Is it a real language?"

"Real?"

"Do people actually speak Doth . . . whatever it is?"

"The Dothraki people in *Game of Thrones* speak it. It's a show. Drogo died. He was an awesome warrior."

"How did you learn to speak Doth-raki?"

"Online. Some guy was hired to make it for the show. They made dictionaries and everything. It's cool." A grin spread across Toby's face.

"Sounds cool. Say something to me."

"M'athchomaroon!"

"What does that mean?"

"It's a respectful way of saying hello. Like, M'athchomaroon Khaleesi Jennifer."

"Nice."

"San athchomari yeraan. That means, ah, thank you."

"That's very interesting."

"Anha vazhak yeraan thirat. I said, I'll let you live." Toby laughed.

"Toby, I have to say, when you're talking about something you're interested in, your energy level goes way up. I can see your enthusiasm. Everything about you becomes more positive."

"Athdavrazar! That means, excellent, like saying this is useful information."

"Ath-da . . . whatever you said." Jennifer smiled. "If we can find a job that captures your imagination, you'll make a great employee. I'll do some hunting." Jennifer drew back her shoulders. "Now that I have a sense of who you are and what your skills are, I'm confident that we can move forward. Let's meet same time, same place, next Tuesday. Okay?"

"Sure. Yeah. Cool."

I'm Listening

"I'm listening, but you're not saying the right things." Shaun struggled to keep exasperation out of his voice. With a sideways glance, he checked to see whether the middle-aged couple at the next table was listening. Across from him, Hailey stared into her mug. The tilt of her face made it impossible to read her expression. "You tend to overanalyze situations," he told her. "I've heard you admit that."

Hailey made eye contact and smiled. Her green eyes shimmered with moisture. She twisted stray hairs at her temple and tucked them behind her ear.

"Seriously, we've known each other for fifteen years . . . since elementary school," said Shaun. "You used to be such a skinny little tomboy. Remember?"

Hailey raised an eyebrow. Her smile widened to reveal a dimple in her right cheek.

"Don't misunderstand me," Shaun added before she could respond. "It's not like you're fat or anything. It's just that you used to be a stick kid . . . you filled out very nicely. I mean . . . shit . . . give me a minute to take my foot out of my mouth. I'm such an idiot."

"I think you're lovely," Hailey said softly.

"Yes. Exactly. I'm downright adorable. So, what's the problem?"

"It's nothing specific," said Hailey. "No single incident or mannerism triggered . . . my awakening." She took a sip of tea and gazed out the window.

"Your awakening?" Shaun let out a nervous laugh. "What the hell is that?" He put his hand on his forehead and leaned in. He hadn't touched his coffee. "Hailey, baby, I need clues."

"Clues? Hmm . . . you called me baby." Hailey inhaled deeply.

A group of four young women squeezed past Hailey's chair. They were carrying stuffed shopping bags that made it difficult to navigate the narrow space between the tables. Their giggles and animated chatter forced Hailey to pause until they passed.

"Clues," she repeated.

"Yeah. What's changed? You've been distant lately. I mean, I understand you're busy with your studies and everything, but . . . I don't know. Something's changed. I just . . ." Shaun brushed his bangs off his forehead. He noticed that his skin was damp.

Hailey looked up. "Well . . . you don't read."

"What?" Shaun realized his response was louder than appropriate. He adjusted his volume. "I don't read?"

"Books. You're literate, of course, but you don't choose to read."

A series of sarcastic retorts raced through Shaun's mind, but with conscious effort, he managed to nod an indication for Hailey to continue. When the silence became uncomfortable, he asked, "What should I read?"

Hailey replied patiently. "It's not a matter of recommending titles for consumption. I'm talking about valuing literature. Experience gained through well-written fiction. Being transported. Fantastical worlds revealed. Courage and honour illustrated.

Ancient wisdom. Exotic aesthetics. The dreams of humankind."

Shaun had trouble meeting Hailey's gaze. He scratched his head and brushed back his hair again with an angry sweep of his palm. "I understand the words you're saying. I know each separate word. They make sense individually, but I can't make sense of the order you're putting them in."

"It's not you . . . it's me." Hailey gazed into her tea. Laughter burst from the foursome of young women.

Shaun leaned forwards and spoke in a harsh whisper. "What is this, a romantic comedy? Obviously it *is* me because *I'm* the one being rejected."

Hailey fondled her mug. She glanced at the adjacent table of giggling girls. They passed around a phone that clearly held a humorous image.

"Are you listening?" Shaun felt desperation creeping up his spine.

Hailey looked up slowly.

"Am I gaming too much? Watching too much sports? Drinking too much? Getting fat? Snoring? Do I smell bad? Did I forget an anniversary? Have I offended your girlfriends?" Shaun caught himself making wild hand gestures. He placed his hands in his lap.

Hailey didn't respond.

"What the hell? Tell me, and I'll fix it." Shaun's voice intensified. He saw customers turn towards him. In a quieter manner, he continued his plea. "I'll read a novel a week. Or I'll join a book club if you want. What'll it take to fix this?"

"We just aren't a good match." She gazed down at her tea, sniffled, and wiped her nose with her paper napkin.

"Since when? Everybody thinks we're the perfect couple. Your parents love me. My parents adore you." Shaun used a napkin to wipe his brow where beads of sweat had become large enough to run down his face. He saw a tremor in his hand as he reached for his mug. "I'm perfectly content with our relationship. What's changed?"

"I need depth." A tear, poised on Hailey's lower lid, was released by a blink. She wiped it away with the back of her hand. "I'm inside my head more than you. Self-analysis is important to me. I believe feelings must be shared. Introspection, metacognition, and reflection are essential to my well-being."

Shaun chuckled. "No fear. I have a reflection. No vampire here."

Hailey furrowed her brow.

"It's a joke. You said you wanted reflection, and I said I have one, like in a mirror, because I'm not a vampire. They don't have a reflection, in a mirror, but I know you didn't mean a reflection in a mirror—you meant *reflection*, like thinking about stuff. I was joking. Sorry."

Hailey caressed her mug and smiled.

"Just trying to lighten things up," Shaun said.

"I know," she replied. They fell back into silence.

Shaun could hear an adjacent couple talking about their daughter's upcoming wedding. Floral arrangements needed to be sorted, and the caterer was difficult to deal with. More laughter sang out across the room. The young women started taking photos of each other.

Shaun wondered whether Hailey had found someone else, maybe that master's student that she was always studying with. He dared not ask the question as he watched Hailey fiddle with her tea. It was a question with no acceptable answer. As bad as it would be to discover he had competition, Shaun felt it would be worse to confirm he was being rejected without a replacement option.

He watched the server, dressed in a pristine white blouse and black pencil skirt, clearing tables. He returned the server's smile and admired how the skirt hugged her hips, then shook his head to dispel the distraction. When he turned back to Hailey, she was looking at him.

"There's nobody better than you," Shaun whispered.

"It's not a contest."

"Do you think we should go to counselling?"

"My sister is coming tomorrow with her van. She's bringing boxes and will help me pack my stuff. It shouldn't take long. I don't own much. I'll be out of the apartment by noon."

"But you love our apartment. You're the one who found it."

"I'm going to put my stuff in storage. Paula offered a room in her basement."

"Are you going to live with her? Won't it be crowded with Nathan and the new baby?"

Hailey began tearing pieces off her paper napkin. She slowly rolled each scrap between her fingertips, creating a small pile of tiny paper spheres. "I'm going to BC to participate in a program at the Lost Lake Spiritual Centre. I'm taking a journey of solitude to deepen my relationship with myself. The program is conducted at a remote fishing camp. Well, I mean, it was abandoned by the fishermen and has been transformed into a spiritual retreat centre. It's a program that draws on the core concepts from the world's great religious philosophies. Participants, we're called novices, are there for a full month. We'll work in the gardens to grow our own food and in the communal kitchen to prepare it. Except during instructional time in the evening, we're to refrain from speaking. There'll be peer analysis groups at which we can investigate our life mission and the efficacy of our pathway."

"What . . . are you talking about?"

"My plans."

"What does any of this have to do with me not reading novels?"

"I was talking about introspection. Welcoming new ideas."

"Cripes. I feel like we're living on different planets." Shaun's voice wavered. He looked at Hailey's neat pile of paper balls and felt tempted to flick them into her face. "As a matter of fact, Hailey, I think I'm pretty good at introspection and welcoming new ideas."

Hailey ceased tearing the napkin and held her breath.

"I've reflected a great deal upon the debt I've been accumulating. There's the new hybrid car you convinced me to buy because the second-hand one I could afford was environmentally unacceptable. And the second-floor apartment in the drafty downtown Victorian townhouse you insisted we rent. I did a lot of thinking about the huge electric bill associated with those leaky windows and the baseboard heating. I thought about the expensive organic greens we eat, and the elite artisan bread that always goes stale because there are no preservatives. Oh, and the hot yoga class you just *had* to register for, then never attended because you didn't like sweating. Or, the sandalwood incense that makes my clothes stink, or the natural deodorant that stains my shirts. I welcomed all the changes you brought into my life."

Hailey seemed frozen in place. Her face went blank. She held the torn napkin in her left hand and a partially rolled ball between her right index finger and thumb.

"Now, I can honestly say that I've heard you." Shaun pushed back his chair to rise. "I hope you find what you're looking for. Say hi to your sister for me. Don't forget to take along something to read."

Late-Life Speed Dating

Number One

Bob: Hello Evelyn. So, is this your first time at speed dating?

Evelyn: How did you . . . ? Oh. Of course, my name tag. Hi, Bob. Yes, my friend talked me into it.

Bob: Thought so. You seem nervous. No need to be. I find that ninety percent of the people here are jerks. The challenge is to weed through 'em.

Evelyn: Really?

Bob: Hell ya. I come every month. I swear to God it's getting weirder and weirder.

Evelyn: I'm not sure how to respond to that.

Bob: Oh, hell, I don't mean you. You seem perfectly normal. But some of these broads, let me tell ya . . . If they're divorced, they're full of piss and vinegar, can't stop talking about how much they hate their ex, and usually that extends to all men in general. You're not divorced, are you?

Evelyn: No. Widowed.

Bob: Widows. They can be a bit desperate. Not you, necessarily. You seem normal, but some widows are fixated on getting another man in their lives. They'll go out with anyone.

Evelyn: Even you?

Bob: Ha ha. I've only tried a widow once, no twice, I guess, but they're too needy. Either they're hunting for a man to look after them, pay their bills, fix their house, take 'em places, or, and this might be even worse, they're searching for a man to look after.

Evelyn: That does sound terrible.

Bob: It's exhausting always having some woman asking what you need, what you want for dinner, what you're thinking. Wears a man out.

Evelyn: I can't imagine anyone needing to ask you what you're thinking.

Bob: Yeah, I don't know why folks try to get into other people's heads. Anyway, enough about that. What kinda work do you do, Evelyn?

Evelyn: I teach secondary school. I'm the English Department chair.

Bob: Chair. That's a funny term, eh? Makes you sound like a piece of furniture. But I guess it's no longer politically correct to say chairman.

Evelyn: Not to mention the fact that I'm not male.

Bob: Chairwoman, chairperson. I think that *man* in chairman means person. Like in *human*. It's generic. It was never a problem until the feminazis got their noses out of joint.

Evelyn: Feminazis?

Bob: You know, rabid feminists. Broads who're trying to deny that there's a difference between men and women. You're not one of them, are you?

Evelyn: Well, I certainly support the concept of women's equality. I think women should receive equal pay for equal work and have the same opportunities for employment and advancement. I think women should be respected and not be treated as sexual objects or the property of their husbands or fathers—

Bob: Obviously. But you don't run around with a sign saying, All Men are Pigs, do ya?

Evelyn: No. I would never make a blanket assessment of any group of people. The men who are pigs shouldn't be allowed to spoil it for the rest.

Bob: Right.

Evelyn: What do you do for a living, Bob?

Bob: I'm a private contractor. I do home renos and restoration work.

Evelyn: Oh, I just had my basement done by Henry's Homework. I needed a leak fixed and thought I might as well turn it into usable living space.

Bob: I know that guy. He talks a good show but has no construction background. I worked for Golden Homes for thirty years before I opened my own business.

Evelyn: Henry has a university degree in engineering, and he brings in someone else to do the electrical and plumbing. I was very happy with his work.

Bob: You would be. His target market is nice widow ladies. Here's my business card. The next time you need some work done, give me a call. I'll cut you a good deal.

Beep.

Evelyn: Okay, Bob. And . . . thanks for the advice on weeding.

Number Two

Evelyn: Hello, I'm Evelyn.

Bruce: Hi. Bruce. Wojcicki.

Evelyn: Nice to meet you, Bruce. Have you done speed dating before?

Bruce: Yes, and the three minutes go by fast, so we need to focus on finding out whether we're compatible.

Evelyn: Oh, of course.

Bruce: If you don't mind, I've developed a helpful list of questions.

Evelyn: Fire away.

Bruce: Do you smoke?

Evelyn: Nope. Never have.

Bruce: Do you drink?

Evelyn: I like a glass of wine when I'm out for a meal or in the evening. Sometimes a cold beer is nice on a hot summer day. I'm not a big fan of hard liquor.

Bruce: So, you'd say you're a moderate drinker.

Evelyn: I guess so.

Bruce: Do you use drugs? Recreationally I mean, not prescriptions.

Evelyn: No.

Bruce: Do you have any pets?

Evelyn: I used to have a cat, but she died a few years ago, and I decided not to replace her. I like the freedom of being without a pet.

Bruce: Cat, eh? How about dogs? Do you like dogs?

Evelyn: I don't dislike them if they're well behaved. I'm not a fan of being jumped on, barked at, or licked.

Bruce: I have two dogs. Dobermans. Shultz and Fritz. They're very well trained.

Evelyn: That's good to know because big dogs can be intimidating.

Bruce: How about your financial situation? Are you in debt?

Evelyn: Oh . . . no. I own my home, have paid for my car, and never carry any debt on my credit card. If I don't have the money, I don't spend. It's a philosophy that's served me well.

Bruce: Okay, then. I don't want to get into a relationship with someone then find out they need a financial bailout.

Evelyn: Fair enough.

Bruce: Do you have kids?

Evelyn: Yes, a daughter and son. Both grown with jobs and homes of their own. How about you, Bruce, do you have any kids?

Bruce: My Ex ran off with our neighbour before we could start a family, so I don't have any kids that I know of. Ha ha.

Evelyn: Oh.

Bruce: Do you like country music?

Evelyn: Hmmm. It's not that I dislike it, some country music is very catchy, but it's not what I would normally choose to listen to.

Bruce: What do you listen to?

Evelyn: I have the radio on while I putter around the house. It's usually on CFOL, the adult contemporary station. I like Michael Bublé, Josh Groban, you know, that sort of thing.

Bruce: Can you dance?

Evelyn: Yes. It's been years since I've gone dancing, but I have a good sense of rhythm. Why, are you a dancer?

Bruce: I like country line dancing. Have you ever tried that?

Evelyn: I've done something like it in exercise classes. It was fun.

Bruce: Do you have any hobbies?

Evelyn: Gee, not really hobbies, as such. I like to read, and I enjoy browsing through antique markets, but I don't have a collection, and I'm not very crafty.

Bruce: You like old things?

Evelyn: I find antique markets fascinating. They have such a variety of stuff, and I'm intrigued by the thought of how many people have interacted with the objects. If only they could talk, eh?

Bruce: Do you ever come across taxidermy at those places?

Evelyn: Sure, there's often a mounted deer head or an animal posed in a glass case.

Bruce: That's my hobby.

Evelyn: Oh.

Bruce: Anthropomorphic taxidermy.

Evelyn: I'm not familiar with that.

Bruce: I stuff animals, usually small mammals like mice, squirrels, or weasels, and dress them in doll's clothes. I make little scenes like a mouse schoolhouse or squirrel tea party.

Evelyn: Really? I've never heard of such a thing.

Bruce: It takes a lot of skill, and it's very creative.

Evelyn: Do you sell your work?

Bruce: No. I get too attached. Can't bring myself to give them up.

Evelyn: So, they're in your house? Doesn't that upset Fritz and . . .

Bruce: Shultz. No, they can tell by the smell that they aren't live animals. The boys just ignore them.

Beep.

Evelyn: Well, thanks, Bruce. It's been very interesting talking to you.

Number Three

Evelyn: Hello . . . Trevor.

Trevor: Hi, Evelyn. Nice to meet you. How are you holding up so far?

Evelyn: Well, you're only number three, seven to go. I guess I'll survive.

Trevor: It's a different sort of experience.

Evelyn: Is this your first time?

Trevor: Second. I was here last year. Met a very nice woman, but she moved out East to be nearer her daughter. So, I thought I'd try again.

Evelyn: I'm glad to hear that you had some success. I was beginning to wonder if this works.

Trevor: It's amazing what an accurate sense of someone you can get in three minutes. People can't help but reveal their true selves.

Evelyn: I'm starting to see that.

Trevor: So, tell me about yourself. How do you spend your days?

Evelyn: Well, I'm a high school English teacher. I'll probably retire at the end of this year. I love my job, but my energy level is not what it once was.

Trevor: Teenagers do demand a lot of energy. I have two kids, and they were nothing but trouble from thirteen to twenty-one. The divorce didn't help. Their mother never set any boundaries. She had no controls on her own behaviour, so I don't know why I expected that she'd have rules for the kids.

Evelyn: How old are they now?

Trevor: Jodi is twenty-eight. She's got two kids, ages five and
           three, with her good-for-nothing druggie boyfriend.
           Poor little shits have had a pretty sketchy start in life.

Evelyn: That must be a tremendous worry for you.

Trevor: Yeah, but there's nothing I can do. Troy is working at
           an auto parts factory. He makes good money but spends
           it all on booze. Both of them seem to be following in
           their mother's footsteps. It's a shame, really.

Evelyn: I'm sorry to hear that.

Trevor: You have kids?

Evelyn: Yes, one girl and one boy, like you. They're both out
           of the house. Both working. They seem to be on their
           way.

Trevor: Lucky you. I guess your ex didn't screw them up.

Evelyn: Oh, I don't have an ex. My husband died. A heart attack
           seven years ago.

Trevor: Oh, sorry. Was he a good father?

Evelyn: The best.

Trevor: That's too bad. I mean too bad that he died.

Evelyn: I understand. I still miss him, but life goes on. I'm here because I've decided that I don't want to spend the rest of my days alone. And I can't burden my kids with keeping me company. That's not fair to them. Now, tell me about yourself, Trevor. Are you still working?

Trevor: Nah. I retired three years ago. Got a good pension and was happy to get out of the rat race.

Evelyn: What line of work were you in?

Trevor: Sales. Insurance and investments. Now, I spend most of my time reading and fishing.

Evelyn: Oh, I'm a big reader. Who are your favourite authors?

Trevor: I like true crime novels. Can't remember authors' names. I like trying to figure out who the murderer is. Some of the stories are really gruesome, bodies hacked up and stuffed in freezers or buried in basements. I love stories that are based on real life events.

Evelyn: Ick, that kind of story would give me nightmares.

Trevor: Nah, most of the time, the killer is someone who knew the victim. It's not the sort of thing that is a threat to anyone else.

Evelyn: And you say you like fishing. My husband was an outdoorsman. He went to BC once on a fly-fishing trip with his university pals. He loved to hike, even took up rock climbing.

Trevor: Standing in the middle of a river is not my idea of fishing. I've got a fibreglass boat with an Evinrude four-stroke engine. I can get up to sixty miles per hour.

Beep.

Evelyn: Oops. There's the signal. Off we go.

Number Four

Evelyn: Hello.

Warren: Hi.

Evelyn: My name's Evelyn, and I see that you're Warren.

Warren: Yes.

Evelyn: How has the evening been going for you, Warren?

Warren: Fine.

Evelyn: Have you participated in one of these events before?

Warren: Yes.

Evelyn: Oh. Do you find it's a good way to meet people?

Warren: Not really.

Evelyn: Then . . . why did you come back?

Warren: I'm on the contact list.

Evelyn: Oh. How does that work?

Warren: They email me a flyer with the dates.

Evelyn: Of course, but . . . is there a discount for repeated participation or something?

Warren: No.

Evelyn: No frequent-flyer incentive?

Warren: No.

Evelyn: But you keep on coming.

Warren: I live within walking distance.

Evelyn: Mmm. Right. That's convenient.

Warren: I mainly come for the snacks.

Evelyn: You like pretzels, do you?

Warren: Anything salty, really.

Evelyn: We have one and a half more minutes. Is there anything you want to talk about?

Warren: Not really.

Evelyn: Oh. Okay. Would you pass me a pretzel, please?

Beep.

Number Five

Derek: Hey.

Evelyn: Hey to you, too.

Derek: So, what're you looking for in a relationship?

Evelyn: Well . . . Derek . . . that's a good question. You're the first one to ask me that. It's beginning to become clear to me that I haven't really considered what my goal is. I'm here because a good friend encouraged me to come. She's married, and I think she really just wanted me to report back on how these things work. You know.

Anyway, I should mention that I'm a widow. My husband died of a heart attack seven years ago, so I've been on my own a long time. Or so it seems. I have a son and daughter. They're both grown and have lives of their own. Don't need me much anymore. At least not until they decide to produce grandkids, I guess.

So . . . I thought it might be nice to have a companion. You know, someone to go to the theatre with, maybe a bridge partner, someone to travel with, I suppose. It's awkward to be the only single in my social group. I throw off the symmetry at dinner parties, being the odd number and such.

Yes, a companion. That's my answer. Someone with similar interests. Someone to spend time with. How about you, Derek? What're you looking for?

Derek: I'm looking for someone who is sexually adventurous. A woman with a good figure and some conjugal skills. I like an aggressive partner. Role playing is a real turn-on for me. I've got quite an extensive collection of toys to spice things up, and with the help of my magic blue pill can keep performing for an extended length of time. Women like that, for sure. At our age, it's nice not to have to worry about birth control anymore, eh?

I like to go bareback, so that's a big plus for me. Of course, I have documentation to prove that I'm free of STDs and expect the same from you. You've been checked out, haven't you?

Evelyn: Gee . . . no.

Derek: That's a deal breaker.

Evelyn: Right you are. I understand completely.

Beep.

Number Six

Stan: Hello, lovely lady. May I take a seat?

Evelyn: Of course. My name is Evelyn.

Stan: And I am Stanford. Stan, to you. How are you faring this evening?

Evelyn: I'm surviving, Stan. It's an interesting process.

Stan: This is your first time partaking in speed dating, I surmise?

Evelyn: Yes. How about you?

Stan: Oh, I've participated a few times both here and in Fort Lauderdale, where I winter. I've met some charming women who have offered convivial company. I like to think that they also found me companionable.

Evelyn: I notice that you have an accent. Where are you from, originally?

Stan: My childhood was spent in Johannesburg. South Africa. My father was in the mining business.

Evelyn: That sounds very exotic. I've never been to the African continent, but it's on my travel list.

Stan: Oh, may I disavow you of that plan. Much of the continent is barren, impoverished, and violent. Not the place for a sweet woman such as yourself.

Evelyn: But South Africa is very progressive. Is it not?

Stan: My childhood there was perfection. We lived on a beautiful estate. My father's mines were productive, and my mother had servants to assist her with domestic and parental chores. I was educated in the colonial school system, played cricket and polo. I have many fond memories, indeed.

Evelyn: Sounds lovely.

Stan: Of course, now it's all different.

Evelyn: How so?

Stan: The city has grown to nearly a million people. The streets are crowded with traffic. Costs have soared, and the Liberals are making a mess of the government. A black president for heaven's sake. My consolation is that my parents did not survive to see such degradation.

Evelyn: Oh. I thought that race relations were good in South Africa.

Stan: Good for whom, my dear?

Evelyn: Gee Stan . . . I thought good for everyone.

Stan: Really? That's a sweet notion.

Beep.

Number Seven

Ted: Lucky number seven. Hi. I'm Ted.

Evelyn: Hi. Evelyn.

Ted: I've never done this before, Evelyn. I'm finding it a bit overwhelming.

Evelyn: Are you meeting any interesting people?

Ted: Well, I've had one marriage proposal.

Evelyn: Really? It was a joke, right?

Ted: I don't think so. Don't be too obvious, but that woman to your left, the one with the bright red hair. She said she could read my aura and that we had been married in a previous lifetime. She explained that, in the past, she was the man and I was the woman. She was sure that our spirits have been reincarnated to bring us together again.

Evelyn: That's . . . gee . . . that's just plain crazy.

Ted: Yes. Yes it is. How about you? Anyone propose yet?

Evelyn: No. I was accused of being a radical feminist, and I failed to make the grade because I didn't know how to line dance, and then, oh, then there was the guy who expressed concern about whether I had sufficient sexual skills.

Ted: Which guy?

Evelyn: I'm not pointing him out. But . . . to answer your question, it has been quite a mixed bag as they say.

Ted: We'll have stories to tell at work tomorrow if nothing else.

Evelyn: Oh yes, I have a friend who made me promise to call as soon as I get home tonight.

Ted: Well, Evelyn, you seem pretty normal.

Evelyn: You do, too. What's the catch?

Ted: I *am* normal. I'm a software developer. I'm divorced. Amicably. Sharon and I got married right out of high school because she was pregnant. We hung in until the kids were launched but didn't really belong together. She's already remarried to a great guy. I'm happy for her.

Evelyn: That's wonderful. Very mature. I'm a widow, myself. It's been seven years. It was fine at first. I kind of liked not being accountable to anyone. I think I'm ready to have someone to share life with now, though.

Ted: Man. That's tough losing a spouse. I hope it was not a long-suffering illness.

Evelyn: Quite the opposite, an unexpected departure. He went for a jog, had a heart attack, and died on the spot.

Ted: That's rough.

Evelyn: Thankfully, he left all our financial dealings in good order. I've heard about widows who faced real problems when they lost their husbands suddenly.

Ted: Hey, I wouldn't mind meeting up for coffee sometime. Give me a thumbs up at the end of the night, and I'll give you a call.

Evelyn: Is that how it works?

Ted: Yeah. They're going to ask you which 'dates' you want to follow up with.

Evelyn: Okay. Thumbs up it is. Nice to meet you, Ted.

Beep.

Number Eight

Evelyn: Excuse me. There doesn't seem to be anyone at my station.

Facilitator: Oh, right. We had one bachelor leave. He wasn't feeling well. Here. Why don't you get a start on your summary sheet while you have a break?

Evelyn: Oh. Okay. Thanks. Do you have a pencil? Cheers.

Beep.

Number Nine

Randy: Evelyn? Evelyn Manford? Fancy meeting you here.

Evelyn: Randy Northbrook? Well, my, my. It's been what . . .
            ten years?

Randy: At least. Hey, I heard about David. It must've been a
            shock to lose him so suddenly.

Evelyn: Yes. But easier than Cheryl's cancer. You both went
            through so much. How are the girls?

Randy: Both married to good guys. Wendy is living on the
            West Coast. They run a little inn just outside of
            Vancouver. Patti is in town. It's great because I get to
            see the grandkids. You know, soccer games and stuff.

            Are you a grandma yet?

Evelyn: Not yet. But I have hope.

Randy: Funny how our paths diverted, eh?

Evelyn: When you moved out of the neighbourhood, we just
            lost touch.

Randy: The condo was much better for me. The house held too
            many memories.

Evelyn: I understand.

Randy: Are you still in the same house?

Evelyn: They'll have to carry me out in a box. I love that place
            so much, it's become part of me.

Randy: Yeah, I understand. I miss the old gang sometimes.

Evelyn: You should come over. I'll make you lunch.

Randy: That would be nice. A bit strange, but nice.

Evelyn: Life does take some strange turns. Doesn't it?

Randy: It does, indeed. You know, Cheryl used to be very jealous of you.

Evelyn: What're you talking about?

Randy: When you first moved to the street. You were so young and fit. Cheryl had already had Wendy and was having trouble getting her figure back. You used to mow the lawn in those short shorts. Remember?

Evelyn: Oh, to be so young.

Randy: Cheryl caught me watching you when I was cutting the hedge. Gave me a right talking to. Geez. That was so long ago. You still look great, Evelyn. The laugh lines at the corners of your eyes, huh, it's a new level of beauty.

Evelyn: I've always wondered why men become so much more handsome as they age. Grey hair looks so distinguished on a man.

Beep.

Randy: Darn. Time's up. Lunch, eh? Sounds like a plan.

Number Ten

Walter: Well, what's your story, ah, Evelyn?

Evelyn: Well, good evening to you, too, Walter. My story? I guess the synopsis is that I'm a widow with two independent, grown children, and I'm looking for a companion. Someone to socialize with. And you?

Walter: I'm here because my daughter nagged me to come. She thinks I've been on my own too long. My wife died a decade ago. Breast cancer. Shitty disease, and the chemotherapy was even worse.

Evelyn: Yes. I've lost friends to cancer. It's awful.

Walter: Personally, I'm quite happy living on my own. It's just fine having no one to report to, being able to do whatever I want whenever the mood strikes me.

Evelyn: Yes, I understand the freedom that you're describing. But sometimes I get lonely. There are times when my friends are doing things as couples and I feel like a fifth wheel. You know what I mean?

Walter: I've never been much for socializing. Give me a good book, red wine, and classical music, and I'm set for the evening.

Evelyn: I've spent many a night exactly in that manner.

Walter: I think making small talk with people is overrated. I don't care about how my neighbours maintain their lush lawn or what tile they're using in their bathroom renovation. And I sure as hell don't give a damn about what sports their grandkids play.

Evelyn: Grandparents can be a bore. I intend to force everyone to listen to my bragging when I get the chance. You don't have grandkids, Walter?

Walter: Sure I do. My daughter who lives in town has two boys, high school aged, and the one in Quebec has a girl in college. Good kids, but I don't monitor every move they make.

Evelyn: Well, I guess you can report back that you attended the event and have determined that your life is just fine the way it is.

Walter: You've got that right.

Evelyn: I think it's wonderful that you're content. That's what we're all striving for, after all. Isn't it?

Walter: Exactly.

Evelyn: And with that, the rotation is done, I guess.

Walter: Has it been ten people already?

Evelyn: Yup.

Walter: The time went fast.

Evelyn: Yes, it did, didn't it?

Walter: It was kind of fun.

Evelyn: Downright entertaining, I'd say.

Walter: I might do this again, you know.

Evelyn: Me too.

No Try There Is

"A problem you have, my friend."

"Yes," said Josh. "I need you to tell me what to do about my roommates." He'd known Newton, never Newt, since first year. They were in the same engineering program. Newton didn't have roommates. Refused to.

"A challenge it is, with strangers cohabiting." Newton interacted with his phone while conversing. He found it stressful to focus on a single activity.

Josh waited until Newton looked up. "I've tried to make it work. Things were going pretty well, recently. Mac stopped eating my food. He's not a fan of whole grain bread and raw veggies. Tony's not using my towel anymore 'cause I keep it in my bedroom."

"Good tactics these are."

"I put a lock on my door like you suggested, and I don't leave my wallet in my jacket anymore. I wish I could get out of the damn lease." Josh took a drink of coffee while Newton responded to a text. "They started stealing."

"I thought a lock you had."

"Not from me, from the grocery store. They came up with a scam."

Newton raised an eyebrow: his most dramatic expression of interest.

"You see, they get a monthly allowance from their parents for rent and food, only they spend it all on booze and drugs. I swear those two are stoned twenty-four seven."

"An expensive habit that is."

"Yes, so that's why they were eating my food. But now I don't buy things they like, so they started stealing groceries. They use two different stations in the self-checkout lane. One messes up the machine trying to scan a couple of cheap items and calls the attendant over for help. Meanwhile, the other pretends to scan his stuff and calmly walks out. They get a week's worth of food for a couple of bucks. They move from store to store and vary the time of day so no one picks up on the pattern. They brag about it."

"You, their behaviour does not impact."

"Is that true?"

"From you, they no longer steal."

"But, when people steal from the grocery store, it's not a victimless crime. Prices are adjusted to accommodate this loss of inventory. Retailers need to implement higher levels of security, another increased cost passed along to honest consumers like you and me."

"Efficient the security is not," said Newton while tapping on his phone.

"If I keep their secret, I become an accomplice."

"What you learned, you must pass on. Their willing confederate, you must not be."

"I know. Keeping quiet makes me complicit. And at the same time, I'm the victim of their crime. It's ridiculous. I don't know what to do."

Newton made a noise that suggested some depth of thought. Josh heard a sort of *hmm* as Newton sent another text but was not sure whether the consideration was regarding the digital conversation or this real-time interaction.

"What do you think I should do?" he asked outright.

"Many options you have."

"Great. Run through them for me, will ya, Newton? Let's do a pros and cons list."

"Them you could confront."

"Nope. That's off the table. They're both bigger than me, and when they're high, their tempers are poorly managed. They'd beat the crap out of me."

"Nothing is an option."

"What? Do you mean I have no options? Or are you saying I have the option to do nothing?" Josh got no response from his companion. "I explained why doing nothing is a no go. Want another coffee?" Newton made a gesture, declining the offer as he picked up his phone again. Josh carried his empty mug to the counter and got a refill of dark roast. When he returned, Newton was smirking. "What's so funny?"

"Between mechanical engineers and civil engineers, what is the difference?"

"I give up. What's the difference?"

"Weapons, mechanical engineers make. Targets, civil engineers build." Newton looked very pleased with himself.

"Hilarious. Are you ready to be of some practical help?" asked Josh.

"Anonymous you must be."

"Yes, but to whom must I be anonymous? Their parents? I've got contact numbers for use in emergencies. Or the grocery store? Or the police?"

"A different level of consequence each one has."

"Yup."

Newton began tapping his fingers on the table. His phone had fallen silent, and his mug was empty.

"So?" Josh was tempted to lay his hand over his friend's to cease the tapping.

"With parents, anonymity cannot be assured."

"I agree," said Josh.

"A permanent consequence, the police would become."

"Possibly. But, if it's their first offence, the court might—"

"Motive would be revealed through criminal investigation."

"Right. But maybe I'd be performing a service to them. Being sent to rehab could save their lives. The way they're going, they're not going to make it through university never mind find a job and get a life."

"Difficult to see is the future." Newton smiled. "A right to fail, they have."

Josh pondered the concept of a right to fail while Newton responded to a text. He wondered whether his own motivation was an ethical mandate to help others or whether this was about punishing behaviour he disapproved of. When Newton's attention returned, Josh said, "I feel an obligation to take action which supports my value system. I want to live in a fair, safe, and just society. Consequently, I think people should be treated in the manner they deserve. Mac and Tony are engaging in a variety of illegal activities. As a law-abiding citizen, I should report this to the authorities before they do harm to themselves or others."

"A tidy rationale this is." At last, Newton seemed fully attentive.

"If I tip off the grocery store, it would result in better security, which would foil future scams, but without naming Mac and Tony, they might never be held responsible for their past thefts."

"It is punishment that you want."

"No. It's bigger than that. There should be a consequence both for their stealing and for their substance abuse. And for manipulating their parents. They're abusing the people they should respect the most. And then there's me. They put me in this uncomfortable situation of trying to decide what to do."

"No try there is."

Although Newton's obsession with Yoda's philosophy no longer annoyed him as it once did, Josh wished his buddy would speak like a normal person. "Now you're just playing head games with me. So, what you're suggesting is . . . I should pick an option and do something, anything."

"Made a decision must be."

Josh reviewed the options while Newton turned to his phone again. His gut told him doing nothing was not an option. Inaction was not fair to society or to his roommates' well-being, so one decision was off the list. All he had to do was determine whom to tell. Their parents were out because they'd try to cover up the behaviour. It had to be either the store or the police. Both could result in the same outcome if he named Mac and Tony. He felt there would be no point in doing anything without naming them. Might as well call the cops, then. They'd keep the tip anonymous. "I have to call the police."

"Not necessary is this action," said Newton.

Josh was bewildered by this response. "Why not?"

"Report them already I have." Newton held up his phone and smiled.

Marion Reidel

The Red Dress

"Did you see what she was wearing?"

"Oh, yes . . ."

"Annie would die of embarrassment . . . if she wasn't already dead." Marg shook her head as she lifted the lid on the miniature teapot. "Who would guess that her only daughter would cause such a scandal?" Marg set the lid back in place and gazed out the window at the busy downtown street. She and her friends had gathered at this café for over a decade. The table for three in the front window was their spot.

"I don't think it qualifies as a scandal." Dorothy smiled and stirred a third sugar into her coffee.

"Andrea always was a handful." Marg felt relief in her arthritic hands as she wrapped them around the warm teapot. "Remember how Annie sent her to a private girls' school? It cost an arm and a leg back then. She and Peter could hardly afford it, but the public school system couldn't handle Andrea."

Dorothy looked across the table at her lifelong friend and draped a hand on the back of the empty chair between them. "I'll miss her. Annie was a real friend, loyal and true. Gosh, we've known each other for over forty years."

Marg pulled a dried leaf off the bright pink geranium occupying the window's deep sill and set it on the side of her dish. "We did a pretty good job of making sure her last wishes were honoured." She poured her tea. The tiny pot dribbled. "My Lord. Can't anyone make a teapot that pours cleanly? What a mess. May I have your napkin?"

As Dorothy passed the napkin, she saw dust motes suspended in the sunlight like algae floating in salt water. Absent-mindedly, Dorothy drew a heart in the dust on the window ledge.

"My mother's Brown Betty was the only teapot I ever used that could be counted on not to dribble. Nowadays, bright colours and fancy shapes seem to be more important than function." Marg scowled at the little yellow pot.

"I read somewhere that dust is actually eighty percent human skin."

"What?"

"Dust. It's apparently eighty percent dead skin cells. People shed all the time. Look at it, twirling in the sunlight." Dorothy gestured to the beam coming through the window, then took a nibble of her chocolate brownie.

"That's disgusting," said Marg as she lifted a forkful of apple pie.

"Makes you think, though." Dorothy raised her eyebrows. They ate in silence.

"I thought the chapel was beautiful." Marg lifted one of the geranium's blossoms and inhaled a sweet rose scent. The plant released another dried leaf.

"We're all piles of dust." Dorothy sighed.

"And the flowers," Marg put the second dried leaf on her plate. "The pink roses were Annie's favourite. I thought the chapel smelled heavenly, like Eau de Cartier." She picked up her mug. "Too bad her daughter had to spoil the ambiance with a red dress."

"Some of the best things in life can't be seen," mused Dorothy.
"What?"

"Like the smell of the roses, the warmth of sunlight, the strength of friendship, or . . . the mystery of the afterlife. Our dear friend, Lady Compassionate Rose." Dorothy took another drink of coffee.

"Did they put brandy in your coffee?"

"What a great idea," said Dorothy. She laughed. "This place has a liquor license. We could toast absent friends. We've lost a lot of friends in the last two years. It would be easy to get depressed."

"Well, I hope I go before you do," declared Marg.

"Why?"

"Because I need you to make sure that neither of my daughters-in-law wears a red dress to my funeral. They can celebrate in private thank you very much." Marg topped up her tea and mopped up the table.

Dorothy laughed.

"I mean, really, who wears a red dress to their mother's funeral?" asked Marg.

"Annie's daughter, Andrea, for one." Dorothy studied her friend. A lifetime of scowling had etched deep furrows on either side of Marg's mouth. "You know, Annie believed in the afterlife. She's probably having tea with Peter and laughing at us silly mortals. I think they appreciated the flowers and those delicious canapés. And . . . I'm sure they understood the red dress." Dorothy watched the dust motes float in the sunlight and pictured Annie and Peter dancing at their fiftieth anniversary party.

Marg sipped her tea and set down the mug. "But not just a red dress, Dorothy, a low-cut, clingy scarlet dress. Annie was the definition of decorum. She raised her daughter better than that." Marg cradled her mug. "Remember at Peter's funeral? Annie wore a beautiful tailored charcoal suit with a classic pillbox hat and the bit of mesh over her face."

I have a photo of the three of us from that day," recalled Dorothy. "She loved Peter ever so much."

"Annie was wearing those vintage marcasite earrings and matching necklace Peter gave her for their twenty-fifth anniversary." Marg touched her own earlobes adorned with faux pearls.

"They made a lovely couple. And their daughter was the light of their lives even if she was a handful. I'll miss talking to Annie," said Dorothy.

"Annie was so elegant, like an actress from a classic film." Marg lifted her napkin to dab the corner of her eye but realized the tea-soaked paper would not do. "Her complexion was flawless, and her figure was trim. If you looked up the meaning of classic beauty on the computer, there would be a picture of our Annie." Marg wiped her eye with the back of her hand. "She was always immaculately dressed, and her manners were impeccable. I loved how her hair turned silver instead of salt and pepper like my crop. The way Annie wore it up in a bun highlighted the graceful line of her neck."

"Annie was very kind," said Dorothy.

"She moved with the grace of a cat. Even in her senior years, she never took on the shuffling gait, which bad knees impose on me. And her hands . . . didn't she have the most beautiful hands?" asked Marg as she inspected her own aged extremities.

"Talented hands. She created lovely stitchery." Dorothy sipped her coffee and smiled.

"Her fingers were long and straight, not twisted by arthritis. And her nails were always symmetrical ovals polished a subtle shade of pink."

Dorothy set down her mug and picked up the brownie. "She played piano beautifully."

"When Annie and Peter danced, they moved like Ginger Rogers

and Fred Astaire. She was perfect, but her daughter . . ." Marg shook her head and looked out the window. "I just don't understand."

"Annie was always independent. I think that's a trait her daughter inherited."

"There's independent, and then there's inappropriate. Annie knew the correct behaviour for any situation. She never misspoke, never caused offence, would never wear a red dress to a funeral."

"Andrea has her mother's lovely figure," said Dorothy. "She seems to take care of herself. Did you get a chance to talk to her?"

"I was far too busy playing hostess. Did you notice all the bridge club members were there, as well as the ladies from church, the hospice crew, and Annie's neighbours? Someone had to greet them."

"Annie would appreciate your efforts." Dorothy took another bite of her brownie and washed it down with the sweet coffee. Following a moment of silence, she said, "I had a pleasant chat with her."

"With whom?"

"Andrea."

"You did? Did you ask her about the red dress?"

"No," replied Dorothy, "but it happens that she told me about it." She turned her attention to finishing her brownie, lowering her head to disguise a smirk.

"Well? Did you explain why one does not wear bright red to one's mother's funeral?" Marg picked up her tea and mumbled. "I never saw anything like it."

"Did you know she had a heart attack last spring?"

"Who?"

"Annie," said Dorothy. "That week she spent in Toronto with her daughter was so they could see a specialist."

"Oh? I had no idea. Annie never said anything." Marg sat up

straight and glanced at the empty chair.

"She didn't want to worry us," explained Dorothy. "She never liked to be fussed over."

"You're right," agreed Marg. "We nearly had to handcuff her to take her for a mammogram when she found that lump. Remember? It turned out to be nothing."

"Anyway, when they were in the city, Annie bought Andrea that red dress. It was part of a fundraising campaign for the Heart and Stroke Foundation."

"It was a stroke that took Peter, wasn't it?"

"Yes, and now Annie's gone from heart failure."

"A fragile heart was her only weakness."

"So, that's why the red dress," said Dorothy. "It was a salute to both her parents. One gone from a stroke and the other a weak heart. The red dress was a tribute."

"I . . . didn't know," whispered Marg.

"Not to worry, my dear." Dorothy took her friend's hand. "For dust we are, and to dust we will return."

Blind Date #2

She was a poet. Performed spoken word in clipped verse. Encouraged me to do likewise.

Customers watched her enter. Hair was green. Bottom lip pierced. Eyes polished turquoise. She moved like a cat.

I waved.

She nodded.

Patrons resumed drinking.

She approached. Slid into the chair opposite. Offered a smile.

I began to sweat. Fetched our drinks. Mine, black medium roast. Hers, chai tea latte.

Awkward eye contact. She called me Bennie. Benjamin's too formal. I called her Bella. Was asked to. Her name was Janice.

She spoke quickly. Had a child's voice. A penetrating frequency. Neighbours increased volume. Leaned towards companions.

She confidently expressed opinions. Sought validation.

I offered adoration. Asked questions. Where's she from? What's her major? Does she have family? Is her roommate nice?

She answered. Hicksville. Women's Studies. Yes. No.

I dropped names. Gloria Steinem. Germaine Greer. Doris Lessing. Simone de Beauvoir. Tried to impress.

She responded. Laurie Halse Anderson. *Speak*. A book, not a command.

I expressed interest. Listened intently.

A first-person narrative. Ostracized high school freshman. Post traumatic stress. Unable to verbalize. Healed by artistic expression. Intertextual symbolism. Fairy tale imagery of rape.

I was confused. Also entranced. Mesmerized by lip ring movement.

She sipped tea. Smiled. Talked.

I drank coffee. Raised eyebrows. Listened.

She makes bead bracelets. Loves kittens and unicorns. Adores rainbows. Eats pizza with pineapple. Lemon gelato. Likes seventies music. Fruit flavoured wine coolers. The way soap bubbles float on a sunny day.

Chatter exchanged. Three hours passed. I heard of travel. Accomplishments. Ex-lovers. Dreams. Precise details. Truths. Fabrications. Her belief in past lives.

She thought we had once been siblings. Declared platonic attraction.

I paid the bill. Walked her to the bus. Hugged. Farewell, sister.

That Particular Grandmother

"Mommy said you're particular." The child broke a large bite off her pastry and forked it into her mouth. She continued speaking as she chewed. "Madison's grandmother let her cut her hair and dye it bright pink, like an anime character. I like candy-coloured hair." She maintained eye contact as she took a gulp of chocolate milk.

"Being particular is another way of saying that someone has standards." The grandmother drank Earl Grey, neat. An oatmeal cookie sat on a floral plate. "Having standards is what distinguishes individuals from the masses. It demonstrates an enlightened level of civility."

"What's civility mean?"

"Good manners."

"We learn manners at school. Mrs. Pettison showed us how to introduce people. She tried to teach us to do cocktail party conversation, but I told her . . . I'm *only* eleven years old. I'm *not allowed* to drink cocktails." The child laughed.

"That's just a term for polite chit-chat, sweetie. The art of making small talk. It has nothing to do with the consumption of alcoholic drinks. Being able to engage in conversation with people you meet is a skill that can be practiced. That's why your grandfather and I arranged for you to attend The Weston-Chatsworth Academy. Other schools overlook such vital skills."

The child sniffed and wiped her nose on the sleeve of her burgundy school sweater. She took a bite of pastry that resulted in a smear of cream in the corner of her mouth.

The grandmother took a sip of tea. "Are you still taking dance lessons with Miss Nikki?" She resisted reaching across the table to wipe away the offensive smear.

"Nah. I don't like ballroom dancing. Boys are creepy."

"But you and Jeremy Fletcher won a trophy last year. Your gown was so beautiful."

"I'm taking hip hop now. We dance like girls in music videos." The child grinned, flashing the white smear. "We wear stretchy tights and crop tops. We're super hot."

"Honey, take your napkin, and wipe the corner of your mouth. No, the other side. That's it. Much better." The pair sat in silence while Maroon 5 sang "Girls Like You" through speakers above their heads.

The child broke the hush. "Mommy said you'd send us to Disneyland this Christmas."

"Did she?" The grandmother raised one professionally sculpted eyebrow. "Does your father want to go to Disneyland?" This was her son's only child.

"Daddy doesn't go on trips with us." Her last bite of pastry consumed, she wiped her sticky fingertips on the front of her sweater. "He likes to do business trips by himself. Mommy and I take the fun trips."

While observing her granddaughter over the mug's rim, the grandmother sipped the now tepid tea. The child had long, straight, silky hair so blond it was almost white pulled into a perky ponytail. She had the habit of tilting her head and smirking when she said something provocative: a miniature version of the daughter-in-law.

"I think Disneyland is fantabulous. You should come with us, Grandmother." She licked her fingertip and began tapping it on her plate to pick up crumbs.

"Fantabulous is not a real word, sweetie. And I'm too old for Disneyland, darling." The grandmother leaned towards the child. "Are you sure that's where you want to go?" She paused until the child looked up. "I was thinking that a trip to Paris might be lovely."

"You mean Paris, France, Grandmother?"

"Yes. Exactly. It's a wonderful city. We could go to the Louvre museum and see all the famous paintings and sculptures. We could ride a boat down the Seine and view the city from the top of the Eiffel Tower."

"I'm learning French at school. *Parlez-vous français, Grandmère?*"

"I only know a few French words, honey, but I find that everyone in Europe speaks English, so it's not a problem."

The child chewed the cuticle of her right index finger.

"The shops in Paris sell beautiful clothes for little girls. We'd travel overnight on an airplane. We could eat dinner and watch a movie, then our seats would fold right down into beds."

"Really?"

"Oh yes. It's very elegant . . . but it's a much more expensive trip than Disneyland."

The child moved around the table to hug her grandmother around the shoulders. "Is it too expensive, Grandmother?"

The grandmother patted the child's back. "Well . . . I don't know if we could take Mommy along. It might have to be just the two of us."

"Please, please, I want to go to Paris, Grandmother."

"Are you grown-up enough to travel without Mommy?"

"Oh yes. Mommy says she likes a break from me."

"Finish your milk, pumpkin. We'll collect some brochures and make a plan." The grandmother drained her teacup and left the cookie untouched. As she stood and tucked in her chair, she said, "I hope you don't mind if it means missing school."

Hidden Motive

She didn't know his hidden motive. Val toyed with the pair of tickets lying beside her mug. He said a client donated them. He doesn't like musicals. Said she should take *a girlfriend*.

Val lifted her vanilla latte. A fern had been inscribed in the foam. She pictured his strong jaw, the scent of his aftershave, his perfectly manicured nails. Uncertainty made her uncomfortable.

Setting down her mug, Val looked up. Foam outlined the upper lip on the face opposite her. She tended to be self-conscious. Such a *faux pas* triggered insecurity. Val gently dabbed her own lips with a napkin as the face mirrored her action.

He'd given her things before, of course. The bracelet she was wearing, those beautiful topaz earrings she loved so much, chocolates . . . thank-you gifts mostly.

Val made eye contact with the face opposite. A perfect listener. Pale blue eyes framed by meticulously arched brows indicating complete attentiveness. Upon closer inspection, fine lines under the lower lids and at the corners of the mouth revealed themselves, as did loose skin below the chin. What the hell? Where had time gone? Val still thought of herself as young. Thirty-eight is surely a woman's prime. Val touched her own face, checking for telltale crevices.

He didn't like musicals, apparently. Although she could remember him saying he went to the community theatre performance of *Cabaret* and had a good time. If that wasn't a musical, she didn't know what was. Val chuckled to herself. She loved *Cabaret*. Thought Joel Grey was awesome but was not a big Liza fan. She had such an odd face, although her voice was fabulous. Val took another drink and looked around the café.

She knew she had a tendency to read into things. His kindness towards her really meant nothing. He was nice to everyone. But she couldn't be blamed for wishing that he'd consider her . . . special. Val toyed with the tickets. They were excellent seats.

A middle-aged couple settled to her left, one empty table away. Val could tell it was a date. They couldn't be married. The man kept asking about the woman's work. He leaned in attentively as his companion shared anecdotes about inept colleagues. Neither of them might be described as attractive. The woman wore a dull grey cardigan that sagged and had pills across the chest. The man was bald. His frames were nerdy, but not enough to make them hip. Val pretended to look out the window beyond them.

She used the pause to reflect on her own status. Not yet forty and still single. Her career had been her focus for the last fifteen years. She owned a beautifully furnished condo and drove a new car. She made herself indispensable at work. Rapid company growth meant she was one of the longest-standing employees. She liked to joke that she knew where all the bodies were buried. She never really felt the need for a man in her life, or so she told those who asked.

The couple had ordered one piece of cake with two forks. Perhaps they were watching their weight. The woman was carrying a few extra pounds and had not picked up her fork, yet her date dug in. Val put her hand over her mouth and pretended to cough as the man took a forkful of cake and offered it to his partner. Such a cliché.

Caressing her warm mug, Val let out a sigh. Companionable silence could be enjoyed so rarely. The woman to her left was still chirping away. Val smiled at the blue eyes across from her. She loved this café. The lighting was flattering, and there was enough carpet and upholstery to absorb the harshest sounds. Val fondled the tickets and conjured her employer's image. She loved the way his dark business suits hung from his broad shoulders, the electric shock she felt when he brushed past her, his laugh resonating through the open office space, and those hands . . . perfect, masculine hands.

Val's daydream was interrupted by a commotion to her left. The man had held his cake-laden fork too far for his date to reach with her mouth. Rather than take the fork from his hand, the woman had placed both her palms on the café's pedestal table and leaned forward like a hungry chick stretching for its parent's pre-chewed worm. The table tipped. Now, coffee dripped over the edge into her lap, and the couple used paper napkins to mop up the mess. The man went to fetch more while the woman slid along the bench, towards Val, muttering nonsense about clumsiness.

Val wanted to offer sisterly advice. *He's humouring you. He doesn't really care about your life. Don't pander to his patriarchal need for control. Eat cake if you want . . . or don't if you prefer. You don't need to fulfill his definition of worthy.* But she refrained, sipped her coffee, and gazed knowingly across her own table.

The man returned with a staff member. The mess was absorbed. The couple departed. Val's coffee cup was empty. It was time to head home.

She picked up the tickets and held them to her lips. And then placed them on the table. She'd known him for almost a decade.

Marion Reidel

His success had been her priority. She kept him organized, on task, focused. She kept a database of clients' personal details, names of wives and kids, birthdays, anniversaries. She never took time off, was always there, totally dependable.

Val looked across the table and sighed. Her pale blue eyes shone, watery with emotion. In the mirror on the wall facing her, her hair was askew. She brushed her bangs flat with the palm of her hand. Her reflection smiled. Val carried her empty mug to the trolley but left the tickets where they lay. For the table's next occupant, an unexpected gift. For her, symbolic divestment.

Like a Mole on Your Ass

It's a misty Monday morning, and Sarah Davis is about to start a new chapter in her life. Having recently graduated with a marketing degree from the local community college, Sarah is bursting with ideas about how to improve the financial viability of businesses she knows nothing about.

She's come to this popular downtown café to meet a Facebook acquaintance and discuss the potential for a non-traditional business relationship. Sarah's excited about extricating herself from her parents' home, and her goal for this meeting is to identify a functional plan for generating sufficient income to do so.

With a wave, Sarah signals as her potential employer enters the cafe. Although they've never met, Trudy Hardcastle's Facebook profile includes a plethora of images resulting in familiarity. Sarah saw Trudy in a bikini at a Caribbean resort, in formal attire at a friend's wedding, and dancing with a beer in hand at a cowboy-themed bar. Today, Trudy is wearing a tailored blouse and pleated dress pants from which spiked heels extend. As Trudy waits at the serving counter, her updo reveals a tattoo of a paw print at the base of her neck. Sarah doesn't know the woman accompanying Trudy.

"I don't mean to be rude or anything," Trudy says as she and her companion take seats at Sarah's table. "I always intend to arrive on time, but it just doesn't seem to be in my nature to do so."

"No worries. I just got here myself. Cute place, eh?" Sarah had waited for forty-five minutes, which caused her to feel conspicuous and awkward, as if she'd been stood up by a date. She tried to make her five-dollar latte last, which resulted in it going flat and cold.

"I don't want to brag or anything, but I helped the owner get planning permission to renovate this building," says Trudy. "It's a fabulous business. They exhibit local artists, and it's always busy. I hold all my important meetings here."

Trudy Hardcastle is the strategic visionary behind Rainbow Pooches Doggie Day Spa. She earned an MBA from an online post-secondary institution, in Australia. In addition to running her own business, she volunteers as communication vice-president for the town's Business Improvement Association.

With Trudy today is her shop manager, Meghan O'Keeffe. Meghan has animal aesthetics training from a community college and is also extremely Scottish. She has been with Rainbow Pooches from its inception. Trudy makes the introductions. "Oh, shit, sorry to be rude. Sarah, this is Meghan. She works for me. Meghan, this is Sarah who I've been raving about all week."

While the women settle into their seats and sample their drinks, Sarah uses the pause to pretend to check a text while actually referring to her list of key points for this meeting. "So, what made you want to open a pet shop?" she asks Trudy.

"Rainbow Pooches is a doggie day spa. I don't mean to be funny or anything, but I would think you'd have done your research," responds Trudy. "We offer elite services to canine companions and surrogate offspring. Tell her what we do, Meghan."

Meghan has worked for Trudy for eight years, is the spa

manager as well as Trudy's go-to gal and, as such, is a key player. "Och, well, we offer a wide range of canine embellishment services. We dae shampoos an' cuts, of course, oor stylist specializes in fashion forward razor wark, alang wi' a spectrum of colourization, hence the name . . . Rainbow Pooches. We hae a full pet-a-cure menu, including nail colour an' gemstone application. Oor boutique has high-end pet accessories imported mainly from Europe," explains Meghan.

Sarah is confused.

Rainbow Pooches Doggie Day Spa was theoretically created to meet the hypothetical needs of pet owners seeking an enhanced level of uniqueness and creativity for their canine cohorts. Trudy hopes to draw Sarah into her orbit to strengthen the spa's magnetic field.

"Again, I don't mean to brag, but we've been voted best pet spa for five years running. We handle three hundred regular clients and had to discontinue taking walk-ins due to the high demand for our services." Trudy sits back and takes a long drink of her cappuccino.

"I studied your website and completed some market research," says Sarah. "It's a very unique business model."

"Well, it was . . ." says Trudy, followed by an annoyed sideways glance towards Meghan.

"Tis no ma fault," says Meghan.

The three women sit in silence, each presumably planning comments to take the conversation forward.

"I don't mean to be funny or anything, but it's like having a mole on your ass," says Trudy. "Only you know it's there, but to ignore it could result in some kind of serious problem."

"Sure, we were in the same class at college, but ah've no spoken tae her in years," says Meghan. "Och aye, we were roommates, but ah didnae even like her."

"So, you're telling me what?" asks Trudy.

"Och, I'm saying ah didnae tell her a thing. Ah didnae knew how she got a hold of oor client list."

Competition recently arose at the mall, a mere fifteen minutes from the Rainbow Pooches location. My Dog's A Big Deal, and its partner operation, My Cat Owns Me, are affordable pet-grooming centres. There's easier parking access, and the overhead costs are lower than at Rainbow's downtown location.

"If what Meghan is saying is true, and I'm hearing this for the first time, Sarah, then what we're dealing with is retail espionage," says Trudy.

The purpose of Sarah joining the Rainbow Pooch team is to diversify their service portfolio and contribute big ideas on strategies and new markets for their trendsetting curatorial pet services.

"Well, what did you think of my market study data?" asks Sarah.

"Did we see it?" Trudy looks at Meghan. "No? No. We didn't see it."

"I put it in a shared Google folder," explains Sarah.

"So, you don't have it on paper?" asks Trudy.

"Gosh, no. I sent it out in advance so everyone could look at it before we met," says Sarah.

"Yes . . . no . . . of course," replies Trudy.

"Let me summarize, then," says Sarah bringing the file up on her phone. "The niche for elite pet care in this town is reasonably small. However, Rainbow Pooches appears to have a solid and loyal clientele. Your social media outreach is strong. Lots of great shots of coiffed dogs on Instagram, lots of Tweets about how much people love your service."

"Again, I don't mean to brag, but Meghan is an expert at personalizing our services for each dog. Aren't you? Of course you are. Every canine client is greeted by name, welcomed, conversed with. The parents feel comfortable they are leaving their darlings in good hands."

"Right. You're selling much more than just a haircut and nail polish," says Sarah. "It's like you're establishing yourselves as a member of the family."

"Right, you've grasped the essence of our enterprise," says Trudy.

* * *

On a different day altogether, the Rainbow Pooches team reconvene on the rear patio at Conversation Café so Trudy's dog, Bosco, a fuchsia otterhound, and Jonathan Marino-Papadakis, an Italian-Greek financier, can join the meeting.

"I know the meeting hasn't started yet, but I just want to say, this is fabulous, and I don't want this to end," says Trudy.

Bosco is curled against Sarah's bare leg and is drooling on her sandal-clad foot, causing discomfort she cannot openly acknowledge.

"So, Jonathan, basically, in a nutshell, the idea is . . . I mean, Sarah, would you like to explain it?" asks Trudy.

"Ah, sure. Well . . . Jonathan . . . we did some market research, regarding people who are prepared to spend significant amounts of money on their dogs. To determine, you know, what their aesthetic priorities are in terms of their pets. And we discovered some very interesting ideas for new services that might capture the creative imaginations of these pet owners."

Jonathon Marino-Papadakis does not own a pet himself. His tendency towards obsessive-compulsive behaviour means pet hair on his clothing results in hyperventilation. His feet are neatly tucked under his chair, out of Bosco's reach.

Sarah continues. "These target pet owners consider their pet not only to be their child, so to speak, but also a fashion accessory. It's important to them that their dog reflect their personal style and be as unique as possible."

Sarah arrived for this meeting with a shoulder bag full of flyer design printouts in order to be taken seriously. She is worried that being situated on the patio could result in them blowing away if she lays them on the table.

"Nobody's ever done this before," says Trudy.

"No, I'm not surprised," replies Jonathan.

"Obviously, I'm still finalizing the details," explains Sarah.

"Yes, of course," says Jonathan.

"I'm not drinking this coffee. There's a bug in it," says Trudy.

* * *

At eight o'clock on yet another morning, Sarah has held her role as consultant for three weeks. With her honeymoon period behind her, she is excited because today is the meeting to finalize her plan for moving forward.

Once again at Conversation Café, Sarah is entertaining the guest of honour while they await Trudy's arrival. Eleanor Watersford is a potential investor in the company's expansion. Eleanor's toy poodle, named Patterson, has been a client of Rainbow Pooches for six years. His chest is meticulously shaved with a bow tie dyed into the shortened fur.

Trudy is engaged in a phone conversation as she arrives. "You want to paint it orange? . . . Okay, shut up. Orange is for traffic cones . . . No . . . Nobody likes orange. Okay? . . . I don't care . . . No . . . Shut up . . . Okay, okay, gotta go . . . Right. Bye . . . Bye . . . Bye!"

Standard greetings are exchanged, which include Patterson, who is peeking out of the shoulder bag sitting on the chair next to Eleanor. Patterson yips whenever his name is mentioned.

"Sarah has a brilliant idea," says Trudy.

"I don't know about brilliant, but I am feeling quite confident," explains Sarah.

"I don't mean to be funny or anything, but getting the two of you together feels positively dangerous," says Trudy.

For Sarah, this meeting is an important opportunity to clarify her future with Rainbow Pooches and demonstrate her ability to create big ideas.

"So, I've given a survey to all the Rainbow Pooches clients. I'm sure you've completed one yourself, Ms. Watersford. What I discovered is . . . the single most challenging aspect of owning a pet—according to our clients, that is—the single most difficult factor is taking the dog out for exercise."

"We all have busy lives," says Trudy. "We can't spend the day walking around parks waiting for our dogs to take a shit."

"Well, owners report that toileting their dogs is manageable, but the long or fast-paced exercise walk is the challenge."

"We have a lot of clients who are overweight," adds Trudy. "The dogs, I mean. Not Patterson, of course."

"Yip."

"Small dogs are less of an issue. They tend to get sufficient exercise around the house, but larger dogs can become lethargic, which results in health issues," continues Sarah.

"And they look like crap," adds Trudy.

Sarah notices Eleanor Watersford is drinking her tea with her left hand while caressing Patterson with her right. She decides the investor's silence should be interpreted as affirmation.

"So, the big idea is . . . a doggie boot camp," says Sarah. "It would include specially designed workout equipment and personal trainers."

"It's not my place to take credit, but isn't that the best idea you've ever heard?" adds Trudy.

* * *

It's a sunny Monday morning, and Sarah Davis has been at the café for two hours, nursing a drink and using their Wi-Fi to search employment websites. She cannot afford internet service at her new studio apartment due to the expense of furniture, throw cushions, and food.

Her doggie boot camp concept was initially a tremendous success. Owners dropped their pets off for a couple of hours while they themselves underwent a spa treatment elsewhere or handled some other essential errand. Canine clients received vigorous exercise via specialized treadmills for larger breeds and gerbil-like wheels for miniature varieties.

Clients were delighted with the resulting slim physiques and the enthusiastic welcome their pets offered when being picked-up from training sessions. The boot camp program seemed to be the big idea that would maintain Rainbow Pooches' client base and generate additional income.

That is . . . until an aquamarine Afghan hound, named Siren, accidentally strangled to death when she lost her footing on the treadmill and became entangled in the harness. The resulting lawsuit ended Sarah's employment contract.

Blind Date #3

Three's the charm. That's what I told myself. After the previous disasters, I had high hopes that The Universe would send me a soulmate on my third try. No set-ups by friends this time. The scientist in me decided to let technology point the way. I'd been on the Perfect Match website for less than two weeks when I met Cyndi. Yes, that's how she spells her name. I know, but you can't hold that against her. Her parents did the dastardly deed.

After chatting online for ten days, I finally suggested a face-to-face meeting. I mean, face-to-face and in person. We'd already seen each other through digital images. There would be no green hair or facial piercing surprises. She looked cute.

She also seemed intelligent. She's an honours English student with a specialty in medieval manuscripts. She never mentioned unicorns, rainbows, or anything fashion-related during any of our conversations. She balanced comments about herself with inquiries about me. She demonstrated an understanding of what I said. Her parents were both professionals, and she gave no indication of mystical beliefs. I felt optimistic.

She arrived exactly on time, and we recognized each other easily due to our online interaction. She ordered a basic coffee with a little cream and sugar, and an oatmeal raisin cookie. Then it started.

"I'm so happy, happy, happy . . . to meet you," she chirped.

"I'm glad to see you, too, Cyndi."

"I think Perfect Match does a really, really, really good job of sorting through profiles," she said. "And the process is fun, fun, fun compared to the Digital Dating site which has tons and tons and tons of boring questionnaires to complete."

What was with her speech? Our online interaction had been concise and focused. I decided it was probably nerves.

"So, how was the lecture on Fifteenth-Century Lyrical Poetry this afternoon?" I knew she'd been looking forward to the expert that her department had imported for the event.

"It was too, too, too fabulous. Dr. Runkenstocker was totally, absolutely, completely mesmerizing." She paused to sip her coffee. "He explained in a very, very, very detailed manner all the metaphors that reoccur and how a piece would mutate as it was passed along from one troubadour to another. It was so, so, so interesting. You really missed something special."

I was at a loss for words.

"How about you? Did you work, work, work all afternoon on your equine circulatory system essay?"

"No. I had it pretty well wrapped up on the weekend. I took a break, played some video games, and I actually indulged in a nap on my couch," I explained. "I guess all those late nights caught up with me."

"I know lots and lots and lots of people who just can't get anything done unless they cram to meet a deadline. Personally, if I pulled an all-nighter, I'd be wasted, kaput, dead the next day." She laughed. "Of course, I don't mean literally dead. I'd just be awfully, awfully, awfully tired. You know."

"Yes, I understand." But I didn't. What was happening? Was

she making a joke? Should I be laughing? Or was it a speech defect that I should pretend I hadn't noticed?

"Hey." She bounced on her chair with enthusiasm. "Do you know what I've been wondering? You know what? Know what?"

I shuddered. "No. What have you been wondering?"

"There's a poetry event coming up next week. I was wondering, just pondering, kind of speculating about whether you would like to come with me."

I made an effort to close my mouth and maintain a neutral expression.

"Before you answer, before you do, before you say anything at all, let me tell you about it. It's going to be wonderful, amazing, fantastic. A group of women, just women, only women will be performing, naked, nude, totally undressed. They've collaborated on a performance piece about gender issues . . . gender inequality . . . sexual stereotypes. It's theatre in the round, like a circle, surrounding the performers, and the poets interact with the audience."

I found it difficult to comprehend the content of her communication. I was too focused on her speech aberration. Was it morphing, changing, expanding?

"I know that poetry is a bit of a stretch for a vet student, a scientist, future animal surgeon and all, but I think it's good, healthy, you know . . . enlightening to step outside of one's comfort zone. Don't you?" She paused, but when I failed to respond, she asked, "Don't you, Benjamin? Don't you?"

"Yeah, I do. I do. Really, I do."

"Great! I'll get another ticket. It's next Thursday night." She sat back and smiled. "Are you excited?"

"Y-yes . . . I mean, yes. Yes, I am. Very excited."

"It's a small theatre, and it doesn't have chairs. We each bring a pillow, or cushion, or mat to sit on. It's a very informal venue."

"Okay. I can do that. No problem."

"If you want to go out for something to eat before the performance, you know, grab a bite, a little snack, there's a great Indian place two doors down."

"I love Indian food. Especially curry. Adore spices."

"I'm so relieved to hear that, Benjamin. I think it's important to enjoy diverse cultures, a taste of the exotic, a touch of foreign cuisine."

"Me too. I agree. Couldn't agree more, Cyndi."

"Okay then, it's a deal, a date, a plan." She began nibbling on her oatmeal cookie. Managed to smile while she chewed.

"I'm really excited, Cyndi. I'm stoked. I'm jazzed. I mean, naked feminist poetry. That's hot, hot, hot." We talked for two hours without any awkward pauses. We chatted, conversed, exchanged thoughts.

They're Trying to Kill Me

"They're trying to kill me!"

"Nana, you're exaggerating. They don't want to kill you. They need you alive so you can pay your rent."

"That woman, the one who's supposed to help me get dressed in the morning, punched me in the side of the head."

"Really? Are you sure it wasn't an accidental bump while she was helping you?"

"Do you think I'm an idiot, Amber? I know a punch when I feel it. She takes things when I'm not looking. And the food . . . is poisoned. Iris was in bed for a week after eating their mystery stew."

"I think you're lucky that someone else is making the meals. I wish I had someone to cook for me."

In this trendy café, patrons gather to pay exorbitant prices for designer drinks while surrounded by original local artwork. The granddaughter, Amber, is filling in for her emotionally exhausted mother. Their table for two is positioned in the café's front window. It's clear that the senior citizen and twentysomething share a strong family resemblance. That sweet young thing must be terrified as she locks eyes with her future.

"You call that cooking? It's inedible."

"And yet, you seem well, Nana."

"Not that anyone cares. Just put the ole bat in a home. That's what your mother wants. She's too busy to worry about me. She doesn't care that I'm starving to death and being tortured every day."

Customers are serenaded by a satellite radio station specializing in light jazz and covers of 1970s hits. The half-filled room holds a reasonable sample of the local demographic, the only missing contingent being the homeless man who can be found reclining on the front steps of the government building across the street.

* * *

The analysis of elder care at Restful Acres Retirement Residence continues while across the room two millennial men debrief a blind date.

"She had a coffin for a coffee table."

"You're kidding."

"I'm not. And it wasn't a fake coffin, either. It was a real, antique coffin with a sheet of glass for a top. I was afraid to ask her if it had been used."

"Where would she get a used coffin?"

"Exactly. It's a terrifying question that bears asking, isn't it?"

"I'm asking you. Do you think she's a grave robber?"

"She doesn't need to dig them up. Just needs to know where to get them."

"I suspect that there are laws controlling such things, Ben. Was that the only issue you had with her?"

"No."

"So?"

"She had a lot of cats."

"What constitutes a lot?"

"Gee, Nathan, I didn't take inventory, but they were

everywhere. On the back of the couch, on top of the bookcase, sleeping on the coffee table. Anywhere I looked, there was a cat."

"You sure can pick 'em, Ben."

"Seriously, what do I need to do to find a sane woman in this town?"

"A sane woman anywhere."

The two young men chuckle in a companionable manner. They consume their artisan sandwiches and turn their conversation to professional tennis.

* * *

Elsewhere in the room, a stern-faced Asian mother admonishes her teenaged daughter. Having overcome tremendous obstacles to emigrate from the Far East, the mother is confounded by the New World values her offspring embraced.

"Principal say you bad girl. You shame family."

"The principal says, not say. When're you going to learn to speak English properly? Anyways, I doubt she used the term bad girl, mother. Principal Cookson adores me. She tweeted last week about our winning Science Olympics team."

"She call me. Say you bully girls. You mean to them."

"Are you kidding? I'm the best thing that ever happened to those brats. Ha. I was just pushing them to succeed. They've got no backbones. No guts. Without me, they're wimps. Failures. They should thank me, not complain."

What we see here is a generational and cultural power struggle. Nobody warned the refugee parent that North American pop culture would be raising her daughter.

"She say you call them names. Not nice."

"I called them pussies, once, which they are, as they've proven by running to the principal. They're soft. If you met them, you'd see it, Mah. You'd be shamed if they were your daughters. They don't fight for what they want. They'll never be the best. They don't have the strength of character that you taught me."

"I not teach you to be mean girl, Nikki."

"You taught me to be the best, and sometimes that demands being a mean girl. I'm everything you asked of me, Mah. My skin's flawless, my hair and figure are perfect. My makeup is beautiful, and my nails are stunning. I get straight As and I could date any boy that I want. My teachers love me. Your friends tell their daughters to be like me. I . . . am . . . perfect. I refuse to surround myself with people who don't demand the same perfection from themselves."

The mother drinks in sulky silence.

"I intend to accomplish much more than you, Mah. I won't be a slave, serving others. Suffering verbal abuse while wiping some old lady's ass."

Her mother visibly cringes at the comment. "I do honest work. Is honourable to serve our elders. It hard for me, but pays for your home, your food, your clothes. You ungrateful."

"Don't lecture me, Mah. If you want to be worried about someone, take a look at your darling son."

That renders the mother speechless. Her mind scrambles to digest her daughter's response. She longs for the defined familial roles of her homeland, where daughters are respectful and principals never phoned home.

* * *

The café doesn't offer table service. The proprietor thinks patrons experience a sense of community if they're expected to clear their own dishes and place them on a cart. Besides, it keeps staff costs down. Still, an impeccably uniformed staff member moves unnoticed among the tables clearing away items that patrons were too lazy, or uniformed, to deal with. Her black pencil skirt and crisp white blouse seem better suited to a high-end bistro. She wears a plastic glove on one hand as she uses a damp rag to wipe the table surfaces. The wood is intentionally battered to create a casual patina.

The server hovers at the table adjacent to the millennial males. She scrubs an invisible stain and monitors their conversation.

"You know, Ben, you could try a professional matchmaking agency. They pre-screen potential dates based on criteria you give them."

"What? And miss all those fabulous experiences. Then I would never have met Ah-lee-sha, the self-absorbed princess with the glittery phone who orders an expensive dessert then makes a show of not eating it."

"Ha."

"Or the one with the facial piercings and a bazillion bead bracelets up her arm. She loved kittens, unicorns, and rainbows, but I was spared having to deal with that because she decided we were brother and sister in a past life, so that was that."

"Seriously?"

"Oh yes, I'm absolutely serious. Anyway, I did go online and met a woman named Cyndi, with the y and i reversed. Her parents must be crazy."

Nathan laughed. He enjoyed hearing about Ben's dating drama. He sometimes missed the excitement of new relationships now that he was married with a child.

"And those parents should have taught, taught, taught her not to repeat, repeat, repeat everything."

"What'd you mean?"

"That's how she talked. I really, really, really . . . admire, adore, love . . . everything about ancient poetry, metaphors, and lyrical thoughts."

"Seriously, Ben, perhaps you should join the seminary."

The eavesdropping server tucks in chairs as she fantasizes about a relationship with the one named Ben. She's watched him on many occasions, each time with a different female companion. Had it not been for her severe social anxiety, she'd have introduced herself to Ben long ago.

* * *

The men's companionable laughter is interrupted by a verbal outburst from the table by the window. The waitress hustles over to the agitated elderly woman and her young companion to see how she might assist.

"Amber, that's her! She's the one! She smacked me in the head."

"Nana, calm down. You're making a scene."

The server sees that the grandmother is gesturing towards someone across the room. Confrontation makes it hard for her to breathe. "Can I be of assistance?" she asks.

"Sorry, my grandmother gets a bit agitated sometimes. She's fine now, and we're heading out."

"I tell you that's the one. She steals my things. She hit me in the head."

The granddaughter and staff member look in the direction of the old woman's gesture and see an Asian woman and teen rising from their table. The Asian woman looks towards the disruption, smiles, and approaches.

"Miss Betty. How you do today?"

"Still breathing, no thanks to you."

"Hi, I'm Amber, Betty's granddaughter."

"Nice to meet you. I am Lin. That my daughter over there, Nikki. I work at Restful Acres. Help Miss Betty get ready in morning. I know your mother, Miss Sandra."

"Help! Ha! Torture is more like it. A monkey would be more help than she is."

"Now, Nana . . ."

Voices are raised, an audience attracted. Lin's daughter is drawn into the conversation. "A monkey?" The teen steps up to the table. The server withdraws with her arms wrapped around herself as psychic protection.

"Just who do you think you are, Miss Betty? Royalty? My mother is all that stands between you and a total loss of dignity. I've heard all about you. You bet. I've heard how she cleans you up when you soil yourself. How she soaks stains off your shirts because you can't eat without spilling. She's told me that you accuse her of taking things, and it always turns out that you've forgotten where you put them. You're damn lucky to have someone as kind as my Mah to look after you, lady. Back home, she was a surgical nurse. Helping old people use the toilet is well beneath her, but she does it so my brother and I can have a better life in this country. You should show a little gratitude."

Everyone in the room is silent. Frank Sinatra croons "It Was a Very Good Year" through the ceiling speakers. One-by-one, patrons look away from the scene and return their gaze to their companions. Conversations restart, at first a faint whisper, then punctuated with small bursts of laughter.

"So sorry, Miss Betty. My Nikki—"

"Don't worry, Lin. No harm done. I'm sure my grandmother understands that Nikki was just trying to support you. This is a challenging time of life for Nana."

"Let's go, Mah." The daughter wraps a protective arm around her petite mother and ushers her from the café while the granddaughter opens a walker and helps the elderly woman rise. Each young woman feels the pulse of familial loyalty.

Marion Reidel

Good Advice

Once again, opinions leapt from Lisa's mouth like popcorn kernels escaping a sizzling pot. Cyndi had been her target. Lisa longed for the self-control she admired in others: their meditative silence and thoughtful facial expressions.

Jasmine's sideways glance caused Lisa's face to flush as distinctly as if slapped. She couldn't make out the soothing words Jasmine whispered into Cyndi's ear as she clamped Cyndi in a one-armed embrace. Cyndi nodded and wiped her tears in response to the injection of breathy comfort.

The email that triggered the drama remained open on Cyndi's phone. The generously proportioned screen lying on the table was wrapped in turquoise rubber and contained what appeared to be innocuous text.

Jasmine stroked Cyndi's cheek with the back of her hand, each caress serving to calm Cyndi's sobs. "I just don't know. I can't figure it out. It's a mystery to me," Cyndi babbled. She blew her nose and placed the soiled tissue on the table. "He was so very, very, very nice. I thought we made a connection, had a relationship, were a good team."

"You only met him two weeks ago." Lisa tried to bring a sense of reality to her friend's loss.

"Twenty-two days if you count the online portion of our relationship, the digital dating, the electronic exchange." Cyndi put her head on Jasmine's shoulder and continued to sob.

Lisa fought the impulse to indicate the undone button on Cyndi's floral blouse, exposing a glimpse of lacy turquoise bra and the fleshy curve of her breast. Lisa strained to hear what Jasmine was whispering.

The intimacy of her companions' posture prompted Lisa to shift her gaze to the window. The café's sidewalk tables were full. Laughing patrons celebrated the warm weather with iced beverages and flakey pastries.

Her unsolicited comments scratched and poked Lisa's consciousness. She replayed the moment. *Every obstacle is an opportunity. Change is good. Things happen for a reason. Someday, you'll laugh. He's not the only fish in the sea. You can do better. What doesn't kill us makes us stronger.* Unwelcome platitudes triggered Cyndi's meltdown.

For ten minutes, Lisa ignored her bladder's demands. She couldn't leave the table after igniting such drama but would have to get up soon.

Jasmine removed her arm from Cyndi's torso, picked up her own mug, and excused herself. As Jasmine departed to refill her coffee, Lisa noticed the glossy black hair draped over the creased linen tunic she wore. She imagined the narrow waist hidden beneath and the firm round glutes.

Cyndi picked up her phone. Lisa wanted to warn her: Don't reread the message. Don't answer it. Turn the damn thing off . . . but opted for silence and a compassionate expression.

"He's going to become a vet. Loves animals. Wants to be a healer." Cyndi sighed and shut off her phone.

"Mmm," was all Lisa could trust herself to say.

"He loves poetry, Indian food, and nudity," Cyndi added.

Lisa wondered how these things might be connected, but dared not ask. Jasmine returned with a coffee for herself and water for Cyndi. Lisa took the opportunity to head to the bathroom. While washing her hands, she inspected her face in the mirror. The fluorescent lighting was less than flattering. There appeared to be dark circles below her eyes and a permanent crease seemed to be forming at the corner of her mouth. A shiver went down her spine—she looked a lot like her mother. And she sounded like her, too. Her mother's eagerness to hand out advice always bothered her.

Lisa returned to the table to find her two friends huddled over Cyndi's phone. "You see, see, see what I mean? That icon means there are men who want to communicate with me. They want to talk to me. Want to find out what I'm like."

"So, why don't you press the button and see what happens?" asked Jasmine. "Isn't that the reason you joined the website to begin with?"

"But last time I got my heart broken, smashed, crushed to pieces." Cyndi looked up as Lisa rejoined them. "What do you think I should do?"

"About what?" Lisa asked, to give herself time to craft an acceptable response.

"About dating, finding a man, connecting with a life partner. Do you think the app is the right option?"

"I'm not sure those things work. You know that Jasmine and I met at the rehab centre. Our relationship grew from face-to-face interactions and shared experience."

"It can't do any harm," suggested Jasmine. "Pressing the smiley face simply accesses more information about the individual. It doesn't commit you to meeting him."

"I know, but that's how it started with Benjamin. We got along really, really, really well online, but it fell apart in real life." Cyndi began to sniffle again.

"What do you think went wrong?" Lisa thought she might be able to lead Cyndi to discover her own insight.

"It could be a cosmic mismatch," said Jasmine. "Your stars may not be completely aligned."

"But he was so cute, absolutely adorable, a real sweetie," whined Cyndi.

"Physical appearance is not as important as compatible personalities and common interests," said Lisa. It seemed an indisputable remark.

"I like animals, and he enjoyed feminist poetry. He really liked it. The nudity didn't bother him at all."

"You took him to see naked feminist poetry?" Lisa realized that she asked this with far too much inflection.

"Are you suggesting there's something wrong with that, Lisa?" Jasmine frowned and tilted her head as a challenge. "I would think it's desirable to find a man who upholds feminist values and is comfortable with nudity."

"I'm sure you're right," said Lisa. "I just feel that nude poetry qualifies as a challenging choice so early in a relationship."

"Better to find out now if he has issues with the power of the goddess. Why would Cyndi want to waste time if he has macho hang-ups?"

Lisa was familiar with Jasmine's defensive tendencies. "He might not necessarily be anti-feminist, but he's certainly a scientist. After all, he's studying to be a vet. Asking a scientist to engage in nude poetry is a bit much, don't you think?"

"But he agreed to go. Said he was interested. Seemed enthusiastic." Cyndi's voice verged on cracking.

"Of course he did. He liked you and wanted to please you. It's called the honeymoon part of a relationship. It's the time when we all agree to do what the other person wants because we want to get to know them, want them to like us. But it can't be sustained."

Lisa saw Jasmine purse her lips. Disapproval radiated from her, but Lisa continued. "Like I said before, things happen for a reason. Now you know that you need to identify your interests more clearly during your initial contact. This Benjamin guy is not the only one out there. You can find a better match. Try to think about the search as part of the adventure. You had fun with him, but it didn't last. Okay, you learned something, right? The next time, you'll do better, and eventually you'll find the right person."

Lisa and Jasmine glared at each other while Cyndi slid her thumb across her phone's surface. "What about this one? He's cute, good hair, nice smile. He likes sports, classic movies, and Italian food. I love pasta. It's my favourite. I can't get enough of it. Maybe he's the one."

Marion Reidel

She's a Landmine

"You're throwing rocks at a landmine. Stop it!"

"But . . . but . . . she's such a . . . bitch." Jarad struggled to keep the waver out of his voice. He was aware of the people around him. He often listened in on private conversations and didn't like the idea of it being done to him.

Nathan took a drink of his dark roast, then let out a sigh. "I'm telling you, man, if you want this to go well, you need to stop poking the bull. Put down the red flag, my friend, and play nice." He'd met Jarad in high school. Despite attending colleges at opposite ends of the country, they maintained a strong brotherly connection.

"Do you think that's what *she's* being advised? Is there anyone telling *her* to chill? No. No, Nathan. I don't think so. She's in full battle mode. I need to respond in kind." Jarad wiped his brow on his shirtsleeve. He wished he'd ordered a beer instead of coffee, but mid-morning drinking wasn't a responsible option.

"Remember, this is someone you once loved. Someone who once loved you. The goal is to mend fences, do damage control, heal old wounds, ah, negotiate a truce, sign a peace treaty, ah . . . I'm running out of clichés."

"Hilarious." Jarad slumped back into his chair.

"No, really. Throwing fuel on her fire is not going to accomplish anything." Nathan wagged a finger at his friend's face. "I'm talking to you as a buddy, Jarad, not your lawyer. The drama has to stop."

"She started it."

"That's your perception, my friend. I suspect she'd say the same thing."

"She isn't an easy woman. You've seen how she is. She can start an argument in an empty room."

Nathan smiled and shook his head. He'd been the one who introduced them. They seemed a perfect match. Both were high energy, aggressive professionals, but it turned out that opposites might be better.

"She's a bitch."

"I know. But she's *your* bitch, so you need to figure out how to handle her."

"I was thinking of hiring a teamster."

"What?"

"To handle her." Jarad smiled and looked his companion directly in the eye. "Perhaps with a grappling hook and a trip to the nearest river wearing cement overshoes."

"You watch too many gangster movies, buddy. Divorce courts rarely find death threats humorous."

The men sat in silence while a mixture of conversations swirled around them. Coffee brewing and fresh-baked croissants scented the café's atmosphere. Jarad's foot bounced beneath the table as he tried to censor his angry thoughts before speaking again.

* * *

"I was the voice that helped him through the fog." Rachel crossed her legs and adjusted her floral skirt to drape over her knee. "Being single won't be much different from my current situation."

Jessica shuffled the papers on her desk and sighed. Offering relationship advice to a colleague was always a recipe for disaster. "Let's run through your list of concerns."

"Complaints," Rachel corrected her associate.

"Treat this as a business negotiation, Rach. If you go in looking for a fight, then that's what you'll get. Focus on the desired outcome." Jessica checked the time. "Do you want out, or are you prepared to do the work needed to save the relationship?"

Rachel wished she could light up a cigarette, thought of suggesting they step outside, but Jarad had insisted that she quit. "We used to laugh until our sight was watery." She took a deep breath. "Our harmony was perfect. We agreed about everything. Everything. What colour to paint the walls, where to eat dinner, holidays, movies, what parties to attend . . . everything." Rachel surreptitiously took a tissue from her bag, dabbed the tear forming at the outer edge of her eyelid, and then made a quick swipe across her nostrils. It had been five years since she moved in with Jarad. "When I moved in to his apartment . . . God . . . it was like a dorm room. Sports posters on the wall, nothing but beer in the fridge, and, ha, he had action figures on his bookcase. Batman, Spiderman, climbing among his political science texts."

"Toys?" Jessica checked the time and picked up a pen.

"Not toys. Action figure collectibles. And you know what he said when I asked about them?"

Jessica started doodling on her desk blotter. "No, what?"

"He said, 'I put those things there so you'd think I'm cool.' Ha! And I fell for it. I thought he was funny, and clever, and . . . cool. Ever so cool." Rachel stared off into space as she revisited sentimental moments. A smile crept across her face.

Jessica drew a pattern of circles, outlined them, and then crosshatched over them. She strained to avoid checking the time. "So . . . it sounds like you're ready to get past this. That's great, 'cause I hafta—"

"Yeah. No. I . . . I . . . I need to protect myself from my expectations of him." Rachel switched her legs. "The reason I'm going crazy is that everything he does, every word he says . . . shit, I don't know." Rachel rubbed her hand across her collarbone.

"Remember the positive stuff, Rach. Forget the fights." Jessica leaned forwards. "Listen, I gotta—"

"Forget? How can I forget being called a bitch? How can I forget all those nights on my own? Or . . . or being ignored at the dinner table, having his back turned to me all night, being blamed every time things don't go his way."

Jessica discreetly sent a text below her desk. "Perhaps a better word than *forgetting* is *letting go*," she advised Rachel.

* * *

"I've got a standard separation agreement here." Nathan took a document out of his shoulder bag. "Even though you and Rachel weren't formally married, the fact that you lived together for almost five years means that, legally, you are considered Common Law."

"But—"

"I know. I know. Separate bank accounts. Separate tax forms. You each had your own benefits plans. Still, it's best to put down in writing how any assets will be dispersed. You know, furniture, CDs, the dog."

"The dog's mine."

"I thought you and Rachel got him at the pound."

"Well, yeah, but I was the one who wanted a dog. I picked Shaggy out."

"Any chance that Rachel will contest his ownership?"

"Shit. I don't know."

"Did she look after Shaggy?"

"If I was out of town, she fed him. But she hated taking him for walks. She went so far as to take him to that stupid boot camp place to avoid exercising him. He's *my* dog. I named him."

"Okay. What about the furniture? You bought that together, didn't you?"

"Only because she said everything I had was crap. She'd been living at home, so she didn't have anything of her own. Rachel enjoyed spending my money on all new stuff when she moved in. She picked it out . . . but I paid for it. It's mine. Most of the CDs are mine. The whole damn apartment is mine. She can take her Adele and Feist CDs, along with all the throw pillows and vases."

Nathan shook his head as he made note of Jarad's remarks.

"And she can keep that stupid dining room light fixture. It looks like an alien spacecraft. She can have that picture of the red bike by an Amsterdam canal that's hanging over the couch, the sculpture of the elephant that's standing on its head, and that dumb birdcage with the candles in it."

Nathan continued to write.

"She can't have the TV, or the sound system, or any of the appliances."

"Did she help pay for those?"

"No. They went on my VISA. It took me a year to clear the debt. She insisted we buy a gas stove with six burners, but she's never prepared a proper meal in her life. Just heated up frozen entrees or dialed for delivery. Bitch."

Nathan's phone rang. He checked the screen. "Sorry, it's the wife. Gotta take this." Nathan turned away from his friend as he spoke. "Hi, sweetie. No. I'm just working through some documents with Jarad." He turned back and said, "Paula says hi."

"Hi back to her," mumbled Jarad.

"He says hi back. So, what's up? Really? Shit. I should've been there. Did you video it? Great. Send it to me." He paused to listen. "Yup. Me too. Love ya." Nathan made kissing noises then clicked off. "Sorry, Jarad, but it was earth-shattering news. Emma took her first steps."

"Really?"

"Up until now, she's only been sliding along furniture, but today she walked across the room to Paula."

"Super."

"I'm pissed that I wasn't there, but she got it on her phone."

"Great."

"Seriously, we've filmed so much of that kid's life there aren't enough hours to watch it all. She's so goddamned cute. I've gotta show you something." Nathan opened his phone, scrolled to his photos, then handed Jarad the device. "Look at this kid. Is she fabulous or is she fabulous?"

Jarad swiped the screen to see Emma in a highchair with orange mush smeared across her face, Emma lying on the floor laughing and waving her arms, Emma asleep on Nathan's chest, Emma sucking on Paula's breast. Jarad handed back the phone. "She's fabulous."

* * *

Jessica's phone pinged a return text. "Hey, Shana and Madison are going clubbing tonight. You should come along."

"Hmm. I don't think so."

"Come on, Rach." Jessica tugged at her colleague's sleeve. "The Secret Passion is the hottest spot in town. Some tequila shots, loud music, and sweaty men will take your mind off Jared."

"I'm too tired."

"You don't even need to go home to change. Just undo a couple of buttons on that blouse." Jessica starting texting her friends to confirm the details.

"Jared was never much of a dancer."

"Then it's a good thing he's not invited." Jessica spoke as she typed. "What you need is to get up close and personal with some exotic guy on the dance floor. Screw Jared."

"His favourite evening activity was watching classic films on TCM."

"Oh, my god. Could anything be more boring?"

"We cuddle on the couch with a smooth Merlot and kettle chips."

Jessica set her phone down. "Okay, we're all set. We'll meet the girls at McCabe's for a quick meal and head to the club. This'll be great. Honest to god, Madison draws men like flies to honey. They do love a woman who's well endowed." Jessica started clearing things off her desk. "Scoot. Get your coat and purse. I'll meet you in the lobby."

Rachel logged off her computer and packed up her workstation. She slipped on her camel coat and hung her bag over her shoulder. When she stepped off the elevator, she saw Jessica talking on the phone by the main entrance. She didn't notice Jarad leaning against the wall next to the elevators.

"Hey."

"What! Oh my god, Jarad. You nearly gave me a heart attack."

"Sorry."

"What're you doing here?"

"I thought you might want to come out for dinner with me. I made a reservation at Angelo's."

"I love that place."

"I know."

Marion Reidel

Watch What You Say

"People are looking at you."

"Let 'em stare. I don't give a sweet crap what anyone thinks."

"Sweetie, please, lower your voice."

"It's this damn hearing aid. It sounds like I've got a pillow over my head. I can't hear myself."

"Well, I can hear you just fine. In fact, my love, I can hear your every thought."

Frank laughed as memories of his wife admonishing his behaviour flashed through his mind. Hushing him in church. Kicking him under the table at dinner parties. Poking him in the side at the theatre. *She's been charting my course for as long as I can remember.*

"It's the sixty-fifth anniversary of our wedding next Tuesday."

"Sixty-five years." Frank snorted and took a sip of his tea. "I don't know how you managed to put up with an old coot like me."

"You weren't always an old coot."

Frank felt the sun drench the table in warmth. He looked out the window to watch a young couple walking past, hand in hand. He found it hard to remember being that young. He felt a tingle, saw his wife's hand caressing his. "I could've been a better husband," he muttered. "I was selfish. Left you to handle the kids, the house . . . everything, really. I let work consume me. Seems foolish now. All those years studying the past. Who cares? What difference did I make? Just more crap for students to study. Another textbook. Who the hell cares?"

Frank's expletive caused the two ladies at the adjacent table to stop conversing and shoot him disapproving expressions. With his back to them, he did not register their disapproval.

"You need to watch your language, lovey."

"Sorry, Myrt. Sorry." He took another sip of Earl Grey. "I'll try to do better." Myrtle was the one who got him hooked on tea. She loved British television, *Coronation Street*, *Downton Abbey*. She used tea as an escape from suburban life. He continued to drink it from habit and because it made him feel closer to his wife.

"There's something I've been meaning to talk to you about, sweetie."

Uh oh. What've I done now? Left the toilet seat up? Made the jam jar sticky? Put recyclables in the waste bin? He laughed. It was easy to laugh with Myrtle. He'd always loved her musical laugh.

"It's your grooming, honey. You need to take care of yourself."

Frank ran his hand across his chin. Five days of stubble bristled beneath his fingertips. He sighed as he swept unruly hairs from his forehead. Looking down, he noticed a hole in his sweater and poked his finger through it. His clothes emanated an odour of fried eggs and aftershave. "I know. I know. You don't need to tell me," he grumbled.

"I just don't want you to look like a homeless person."

Tears often gathered in Myrt's eyes when she was saying something heartfelt, but instead of feeling repentant, anger boiled so fast he couldn't contain it. "What the hell does it matter what I look like? Whoever said clothes make the man was an idiot. *Vestis virum reddit.* That's bullshit. Have I ever given a fig about appearance as long as you've known me, Myrt? Have I? You know what Samuel Langhorne Clemens said. 'Clothes only make the man because naked people have little or no influence in society.' Or something like that. Ha! Why would I suddenly be concerned about impressing others at the ripe old age of eighty-nine?"

"Honey, you're shouting."

"I don't give a damn. I'm fed up. Just plain tired. Tired of people. Tired of life. I don't give a good goddamn what anyone thinks of me. I've been on this planet long enough that it's earned me the right not to care." Frank dropped his forehead into his hands and focused on breathing. Myrtle had taught him to breathe deeply when he felt frazzled. She was a big yoga fan and attended lots of mindfulness workshops. He used to think it was all hooey, but the breathing thing really worked.

"You feeling a bit better, lovey?"

"I'm fine. I don't mean to make a fuss." *It's just that . . . sometimes I feel overwhelmed. I used to be in charge, Myrt. People used to come to me for information, for advice. Now, I can't remember where I put the car keys, and I forget to pick up groceries. I look in the mirror and wonder, who is that man? What does he want from me?*

Myrtle was expert at taking patient pauses. It was a trick she'd learned, a way to avoid leaping to judgment or problem solving. It gave the other person space to express their feelings. He liked it.

"You know, Myrt," Frank whispered. "I think we're all assigned expiry dates. My best-before date feels well past. I don't think I'm capable of making a meaningful contribution to the world anymore."

Myrtle often cupped both hands around her mug as if she needed to draw warmth from it. Frank adopted this action and felt the pleasing sensation of heat travel through his palms and up to his wrists.

His mind whirred. *The other day, when I took out the garbage . . . I noticed that there were fewer bags. I congratulated myself on doing a good job cutting down, saving the environment, thought David Suzuki would be proud, then I remembered that I hadn't eaten lunch. There was no cereal in the cupboard at all.*

That bloody neighbour was cutting his grass. He's always making noise like hedge trimmers and leaf blowers. I used to hear birds in our backyard. Now, there's always a machine running. And that kid across the street is working on a hot rod. What's that about? Does he think it's 1952? He's forever revving the engine, but the car never goes anywhere. I don't know why his parents put up with it. They have to park in the street.

That's if the neighbourhood brats aren't playing road hockey. When I was a kid, we'd yell, "Car!" and everyone would scamper out of the way. God this chair is uncomfortable. My butt hurts. These days, kids dare you to run them over. They expect you to ride up the curb. I blame the parents. Kids are indulged.

You should see the colour that Bob Kipling painted his garage door. It's red as a clown's nose for heaven's sake. Might as well paint a bull's eye on it. His wife probably picked the colour to match her lipstick or some goddamned thing. She's a piece of work, that one is. Strutting around in those high-heeled shoes, forever bringing bags home from the mall.

"I don't know what this world is coming to, Myrt. The neighbourhood's changed. It used to be so friendly. Now, nobody gives a good goddamn about anyone but themselves."

"Excuse me, sir. My friend and I are trying to have a nice visit. Could you please moderate your language? Show some respect for others."

Frank turned and sneered at the women sitting at the next table. *Nosey bitches. What are they doing in a coffee shop in the middle of the day anyway? They're too old to be stay-at-home moms and too young to be retired. They should be at work somewhere instead of living off the income of some poor sod who's slaving in an office all day to generate the funds for fancy lattes. Nosey judgmental bitches.*

"I never worked."

"What's that?"

"I never worked. Even after the kids went to school, I stayed home."

Frank responded in a muted mutter. "That's different, Myrt. You were working even though you were home. You did all the household stuff, the cleaning, cooking, finances, even the gardening. You never hung out in coffee shops harassing tired old men."

"I wish you'd take better care of yourself."

"Why should I change?"

"I love you, sweetie. Be happy."

A café staff member circulated, chatting to customers while collecting empty plates and cups. When she approached the two ladies seated next to Frank, one whispered to her. "What's up with the old guy? He's talking to himself."

"Oh, Frank? He's a regular, sort of eccentric."

"He looks like a vagrant."

"Oh gosh, no. He's a retired university professor of some kind. History, or politics, or something. He's been a regular customer as long as I've worked here."

"So, he's not crazy or dangerous."

"My goodness, no. Just sad, I think. His wife died a few months ago. He really misses her."

Marion Reidel

Blindsided

"May I sit here?"

"Ah . . . sure . . . ," she says.

I hope she doesn't think I'm a creep. We're the only two in this section, but she picked my favourite spot. She won't even know I'm here. Ahh. I like bench seating with my back to the wall. Better to observe others, more room to spread out, and easier to reach the outlet. Only problem is that huge mirror. I can see the two of us as if we're part of the artwork. Hey, she's cute.

"Nice to spend time alone, eh? I wasted months in pursuit of the perfect partner, and it's time to withdraw from the game." That's confident, clear that I'm not trying to make a move on her.

"I hear you."

Ah ha. A kindred spirit. Looks as if she's doing schoolwork. "You here alone, too?"

"Blissfully so."

What caused me to ask that? It's pretty obvious she's alone. Her gear's on the opposite chair. I must seem predatory. Sounds as if she's experienced dysfunctional relationships. Or perhaps that was a polite brush-off. I should leave her alone. "I decided that it's not my priority to find a partner. I'm not going on any more blind dates." What made me say that? Now she's looking at me as if I'm insane.

"I beg your pardon?"

Crap! I hadn't noticed the earbuds. This is awkward. "Like you, I'm very busy with my studies. I have lots of friends to socialize with. And . . . I can handle my own sexual gratification, thank you very much."

"You're welcome."

Shit! What'd I say? I can handle my own sexual gratification! Who says that to a stranger? My own sexual gratification! Jesus. At least she smiled. She hasn't made a move to escape, so she must know I'm not dangerous. But, she's put the earbuds back in. Shut up, Benjamin. Leave her alone. I can handle my own sexual gratification. Just shoot me now. Shit! I can't leave. That'd be even more creepy. Look busy. Great, here's my lunch.

"Chicken Caesar wrap and kettle chips?"

"That's me."

"Can I get you anything else?"

"No, that's great. Thanks." Now, try to eat without making a mess. She's got me in her peripheral vision. Oh no. She closed her laptop and removed her earbuds.

"Hey, my name is Samantha, but you can call me Sammy. Everybody does, except my father. He calls me Turd. Just his little joke."

She's holding out her hand. What does she want? Give it a shake, firm, but don't crush her. Gosh, she's got tiny bones. "Hi, Sammy. I'm Benjamin." Turn to face her. Not full on. Not confrontational. Just a three-quarter turn. Show interest, but don't be intimidating.

"Nice to meet you, Benjamin."

She's mirroring my posture. I read in *Psychology Today* that's supposed to show compatibility, but she could be faking. Could be intentionally copying me in order to manipulate me subliminally. What if she read the same article?

"... problems with relationships, Ben?"

"I beg your pardon. I drifted off for a second there." Why'd I confess that? Idiot! Focus.

"Really? You find it difficult staying attached to the present moment?"

She's smiling. Not mocking. Seems amused, not judgmental. "It's just that . . . well, you're sitting in exactly the same position as me. Like a mirror image." What a jerk. Should've lied and said I was trying to remember something.

"Sorry."

See, now she's repositioning herself. Way to alienate her.

"I do that sometimes, Ben. It's not on purpose. No offense intended."

"None taken." She smells like . . . vanilla? Do I have Caesar dressing in the corner of my mouth?

"You know what's really bad? Sometimes, if I'm talking to a person with an accent, I start talking with the same speech pattern."

"Really?" She's flawed. I like that.

"Yeah. Once, I was chatting with an old lady on the bus. She had this great British accent, and suddenly there I was, chatting away in a matching manner."

"Did she get angry?" We are both sitting with an elbow on our table and our chins propped in our palms. Don't move. Don't say anything.

"No. That's the funny thing. She asked me where I was from. She thought I came from the same district as her. I was so glad when we arrived at her stop because I wasn't sure I could keep it up."

"You must be very in tune with people's vibrations." What the fuck? I sound like a New Age jerk. Shut up, and just let her talk.

"Yeah. Exactly. I kinda sense people."

God, she's got a beautiful smile. Okay, she's shifted posture, so I can move, too. Do something different. "Do you know anything about veterinary medicine?" What the hell made me ask that?

"No. But I love animals."

What a great laugh. Genuine. Not judgmental at all. That's adorable. She's listing every pet she's ever owned. I don't need to tell her that I specialize in large animals, farm stock. Kittens are cuter. She does smell like vanilla, and her eyes . . . what colour is that? Burnt umber? Maybe they're contacts. Uh . . . she's stopped talking. "This social interaction is taking some surprising turns." Why did I blurt that out? I gotta keep the commentary inside my head.

"Unexpected is good. You're a quirky fellow, my new friend, Benjamin." She punches me lightly on the upper arm.

"A recent blind date said I was socially awkward." Well, that statement should prove it. Thank God she laughs.

"Everyone is socially awkward. All my friends suffer from anxiety disorders or depression. I think it's part of being human."

God she smells good. Like a cookie right out of the oven. "You smell delicious." Shit! Must I express every thought? She's sniffing her hand. Oh my God, she's reaching for her backpack. She's leaving. I offended her.

"It's funny. I'm immune to it."

What's that tube? She's reaching for my hand.

"It's vanilla hand cream from Body Basics. Open your palm. Here. Now, rub your hands together. Get the backs, too. Rub it all in."

It feels creamy. "I feel like a I'm prepping for surgery." I bet her skin is soft.

"Now, smell your hands."

"Smells great. Like grandma's cookies." Do men use scented

hand cream? I need to stop smelling my hands, or the couple that just walked in will think I'm strange. Who am I kidding? I *am* strange. I'm letting this beautiful woman sniff the back of my hand. Shit! My cuticles are gnawed ragged. Her hands are tiny, graceful . . . perfect.

"Now, you're delicious, too."

"Ah . . . thanks." Now what? The pressure to continue coherent conversation is squeezing my bladder. I'm going to wet myself. What should I say? She's used a magical cream to bind us together in a cocoon of intoxicating aroma. Magical cream? Intoxicating aroma? Jesus. The fragrance must be making me hallucinate.

"So, Benjamin, what inspired your dedication to animals?"

I haven't blown it yet. "I had a dog as a kid. Goober. He was a chocolate lab. Big goofy guy, but the best friend any kid could want. He followed me everywhere and was thrilled to see me when I got home from school. They say a dog is the only thing on Earth that loves you more than it loves itself."

"So, you decided to work with dogs?"

"I started there but have moved to larger species. I'm in my third year at the Vet College. But . . . most girls don't particularly want to hear about my studies. The dissections are too gruesome."

"Oh, in your experience what do most girls want to talk about?"

This question is a trap. She's probably a feminist. Is she being playful or malicious? "Sammy, my experience with women is not to be relied upon."

"C'mon, Benji. Spills yer guts. I know youse gots da info I needs."

She's pointing her finger at me like a gun. Oh shit. Here goes . . . "Okay, copper, I'll tell ya." Hands up, palms forward in front of my chest. "Ya see, goils likes soiten tings. They likes rainbows, 'n' kittens, anyting pink, 'n' phones with gems on 'em. Ya know. Glittery stuff. That's what they likes." Oh my God. Can I pull this off? "Oh, yeah. They likes attention, too. Likes bein' in the middle a tings. Bein' in the spotlight. Ya know. All eyes on them. And speakin' ah eyes, they likes paintin' them eyes wit black lines. Yeah. That's what goils likes. Yeah." Okay, she's laughing. So loudly that couple across the room turned to check us out.

"Oh, Benjamin. My poor, poor Benjamin. I think you've been dating raccoons, not women."

I can't believe how comfortable it is to laugh with this woman. Listen to her. She's perfect.

"So, Benjamin, I'm a student at the university, too. Urban planning. I think human systems are fascinating."

"Ha. Country boy meets urban girl, eh?"

"Yes, but alas, a country boy who declares that he has withdrawn from the game . . . and can handle his own sexual gratification . . . or so I hear."

It's going to take all my willpower not to fall in love with Sammy right now. Who am I kidding? I think I already have.

Writer's Craft

The fortuneteller gazed into her crystal orb . . .
A bouquet of dead roses sat on the table . . .
She contentedly sipped her coffee until . . .

Hannah stared at her laptop's screen. A sea of voices washed over her, brushing snippets of conversations across her awareness. " . . . then she called him back and told him to piss off . . ." " . . . never seen such a beautiful baby . . ." " . . . feel like ending it right this minute. I've had enough . . ."

She kept her eyes on the backlit words floating in front of her. What made her think she could be a writer? Story prompts held no magic today. She didn't give a damn about the fortuneteller or dead roses. She typed . . .

Just write. Write. It doesn't matter what you create as long as you are crafting words. Constructing sentences. Avoid self-judgment. Don't go back and change anything. Allow thoughts to flow freely. Eventually, creative ideas will come. Eventually, a story will emerge. Eventually, my ability to write will develop. Such crap!

This was the message her professor continually espoused. Hannah needed to get past the intimidation of the blank screen. Write anything and see what evolves, he said. Don't go back. No deletes. Revise later.

> I'm sitting here in this lovely café. It smells of warmth . . . happiness . . . no, it smells of congeniality. Nice. Words flutter through the air like butterflies . . . No, that's too cliché. Words drift . . . No, the conversations are more animated. Words dart about the room, some striking intended targets, while others miss their mark. Yeah, I like that.

Hannah smiled. She looked up as a middle-aged couple bumped past her table. The woman offered an apology for the disruption, but the man was unaware of his impact.

> The tiny space was . . . Patrons were packed into the tiny space like sardines . . . argh . . . The café patrons gathered like insects in a hive. What does that mean? There's a suggestion of business, of animated activity, of cooperation, some level of agreed social convention. Then say that. Unspoken social conventions . . . Their commitment to unspoken social conventions permitted the patrons . . . nice alliteration . . . Their commitment to unspoken social conventions permitted the patrons to interact . . . cooperatively . . . shit . . . congenially . . . said that . . . coordinately? Is that even a word? . . . cooperatively, despite the confined space. Okay, what have I got?

Hannah did a copy and paste to gather the words that seemed to resonate most effectively. She took a drink of her coffee and a bite of the salted toffee cookie while she read.

> The café smells of congeniality. Words dart around the room, some striking intended targets, others missing their mark. Their commitment to unspoken social conventions permits patrons to interact cooperatively, despite the tight space.

Hannah could not decide, present or past tense?

> The café smelled of congeniality. Words darted around the room. Some struck intended targets, while others missed their mark. Their commitment to unspoken social conventions permitted the patrons to interact cooperatively, despite the tight space.

Laughter made her turn. At an adjacent table, three young women inspected recent purchases. Silky bits of tissue-wrapped apparel were extracted from branded bags. When their laughter subsided, they took photos, and each of them began typing on their own personal device. She thought these girls made interesting characters.

> Despite the social nature of their location, the impeccably groomed millennial females tweet indications of their social status to imagined admirers. Instead of sharing anecdotes, they post images to Instagram and call it interaction.

The trio of twenty something females disrupted the sedate atmosphere with a burst of youthful laughter. The group's alpha, a pristine blonde with a flawless complexion and bright red lips, passed a pink cellphone to her companions. It displayed an image . . . It held an image . . . It contained an image of . . . a fat girl.

Hannah paused. The idea that all beautiful young women were bullies seemed trite. What might they be looking at? She did a quick image search for the top Instagram females. Selena Gomez 133 million followers, Ariana Grande 117 million and Beyoncé 111 million. What would that degree of celebrity do to a person?

The urban princesses found an Instagram site titled "Fabulous ends with US!" They were supporters . . . believers . . . advocates . . . They advocated extreme entitlement, each feeling assured that she was indeed the centre of the universe.

The young women at the table Hannah was observing broke into giggles and started taking selfies. They leaned their heads together, made pouty faces, inspected the results, and laughed.

Absorbed with their own beauty . . . their own perceived beauty . . . the trio of self-proclaimed royalty captured images of themselves for digital distribution to their subjects. Oblivious to others' perception, obvious self-absorption fuelled their interaction. Oblivious/obvious . . . I like that. Note: add physical descriptions. They're all wearing pink with similar shades of blond hair. Coincidence? I think not. Did their commonality draw them together like some species indicator, or is their symmetry chemically produced? Hmm. I could pursue that. Note: What if one of the trio was a woman of colour, but also had blond hair?

Hannah noticed a bearded man across the room sitting alone, like her. Nothing says "I have style" like a hoodie, cargo shorts, socks, and sandals. His shirt bore the words Women's Rugby. Odd. He appeared in his sixties. His grey beard seemed poorly groomed. Her imagination painted him as a creepy character to be hanging around with female rugby players even if those gals can be butch. As she contemplated his identity, three rugby players, complete with matching team jackets, join him.

He was a human island among the bustle of the busy coffee shop. Alone at a table for four, headphones forged his isolation. His ZZ Top beard draped over a hoodie proclaiming him to be the Property of the Women's Rugby Team. A woollen toque starkly contrasted knee-length cargo shorts and sandals. He appeared devoid of colour, or facial expression. Suddenly . . . cliché, fix it later . . . three vibrant young women arrived at his table. Matching varsity jackets identified them as athletes. Brunette ponytails bobbed, and headphones disappeared as connections crisscrossed the table.

Note: This has potential. Contrast of the three giggling blondes and the brunette athletes. Maybe there should only be two rugby players, rather than three again. Also, parallel the true interaction versus the digital nonsense.

Hannah drank her coffee and ate her cookie as she scanned the room. She felt energized. What other characters occupied the adjacent tables? Last week, her instructor said, "The best thing about writing is that it's free, and ideas are endless." She took smooth, even breaths, ensuring a neutral expression. For her, writing didn't offer freedom. She referred to writing as a sadist, torturing her with incomplete scenarios and elusive phrases. It got a laugh from her classmates, a raised eyebrow from the instructor.

Across the room, Hannah spied another solo patron. An elderly woman broke pieces off her cookie and set them down beside her. Hannah watched this confusing behaviour then realized the woman had something in a large satchel on the bench to her right. She turned to speak to it, seemed to stroke it. There was a high-pitched *yap* and the person seated beside the old woman turned with a smile to make a comment. It was a dog. The old gal had some miniature canine in her purse. Hannah popped the last bit of her own cookie into her mouth and returned to her keyboard.

> A well-dressed old lady hides a little dog in her purse. Who is she? Why does she need the constant company of this petite puppy? What if she's not a sad and lonely old woman? What if she's not what she seems at all???? Ha!

> As the airport express's doors swoosh shut behind her, Molly strokes the furry head projecting from her handbag. It's a short walk from the bus stop to the check-in counter, and she evaluates her reflection in the plate glass window as she enters the terminal. She's delighted to step out of the hot humid air into the terminal's chilled environment.

> At the counter, she flirts with the twentysomething clerk. Molly's old enough to be his mother, so her fluttering eyelashes and girlish giggles are perceived as amusing rather than provocative.

The impending security check makes Molly's knees go weak. Giving her Pekinese another stroke, she straightens the bow fastened to its brow. She shortens her stride and lets her posture slump as she steps up to the conveyor belt. Affecting a confused demeanour, she asks whether her "Snookie" needs to go through the X-ray machine. When the guard offers to do a manual search, Molly covertly gives the dog a severe pinch before handing over the bag. As she hoped, the dog's agitation intimidates the inspector, and his assessment of the bag is cursory at best. Once beyond the security guard's view, Molly returns to her confident stride and gives the Pekinese a massage behind its ears. She smirks at the thought of cashing in the cocaine concealed in the bag's false bottom. "Good Snookie."

Hannah leaned back and smiled. She was enjoying the game. It reminded her of a Simon & Garfunkel lyric. Something about a bus ride and guessing the identities of the fellow passengers. She searched for her next target. Across the room sat a middle-aged man with two young children: a boy and a girl. Where was the mother? Perhaps he's a divorced dad spending an awkward assigned weekend with the children. The boy, around eight or ten, looked surly.

Another weekend with Dad. Why should my parents' breakup disrupt my social life? Does a kid sound like that? I don't think so. He's too young to speak like that, or perhaps he's just small for his age. He's a string bean. He probably gets bullied. All his classmates hit puberty, sprung up in height, sport peach fuzz on their chins, while this kid, this little fly of a kid, is stuck in a child's body.

I hate my nickname. Like it isn't bad enough being the smallest kid in class, now everyone calls me "Mosquito" just to torment me. Damn my short parents. If they had to be short, why couldn't they be small enough to be "little people." That's trendy. That Lannister guy on *Game of Thrones* is sic, and he's a dwarf, but nooooo, my parents are just plain short. My gene pool is wading depth. My inheritance is petty change. Note: find a bunch of short puns for here.

I'm front and centre in every class photo. Stick the cute little *mosquito* behind the sign saying Grade 8. My pal Trevor is amused that he can lean his elbow on the top of my head. He laughs because I stand on my toes to use the stupid water fountain. I can't reach anything on the top shelf of my locker, so my books are in a pile at the bottom. When winter comes, my boots make my notes mucky.

There isn't a hope in hell that a girl will ever dance with me in public. I miss all the funny jokes because they go over my head, literally. I'm just the little mosquito, buzzing around the periphery of the in-crowd's social circle.

Dad says, be patient, a growth spurt will come along, but an evaluation of him and grandpa suggests the chance of me growing much beyond 5¢6² is remote. I hope I don't catch "small man syndrome." Apparently to compensate for the masculinity lost from lack of height, short adult men are pushy and obnoxious. Note: Would a kid talk like that?

Ha! Maybe that would be suitable for the old mosquito, too. There certainly are some people I would like to take a bite out of. People better watch their step. Deadly diseases are carried by mosquitos, like malaria and Ebola. They better beware. Nice. I like the disease metaphor. This kid could be seriously evil, yet never suspected due to his size.

A ping on Hannah's phone alerted her to the time. Her writing class started in forty-five minutes, and it would take half an hour to get to campus. She packed up. Laptop unplugged, journal and pens gathered, everything into her knapsack. It had been a productive afternoon. She incubated several potential scenarios and, thank God, would have something to share. She wondered whether the stress of a deadline was what she needed to ignite her writing, or whether this quaint café was the inspiration she'd been seeking. She liked the Conversation Café and decided to make it a regular hangout. If her own life was too boring to inspire creativity, she'd feed off these unsuspecting café customers.